Roots

Author

Dr. Dinesh Srivastava

rg books

Anybook

Roots (Short stories) *by* Dr. Dinesh Kumar Srivastava

Published By :

Redgrab books
942, Mutthiganj, Allahabad - 211003
Website : www.redgrabbooks.com
E-mail : contact@redgrabbooks.com

&

Anybook
G 248, 2nd floor, Sector 63
Noida - 201301, U.P.
Website : www.anybook.org
E-mail : contactanybook@gmail.com

ISBN : 978-93-87390-32-4
Cover design : Shree Computers, Allahabad
Edition : First, Paperback, May 2018

About the Author

Dr. Dinesh Srivastava

Born in village Awar, Pratap Garh, Uttar Pradesh, 1952. Early education at village school and neighbouring city of Pratap Garh. Shifted to Allahabad in 1964 and obtained B. Sc. from University of Allahabad in 1970. Selected into Training School of Department of Atomic Energy in 1970 and joined Bhabha Atomic Research Centre as Scientific Officer in 1971. Ph. D. (1979) from University of Bombay. Moved to Variable Energy Cyclotron Centre at Kolkata in 1979, from where he retired as a Director and Distinguished Scientist in 2016. Held visiting positions of one to two years in Germany, USA, and Canada, and for shorter durations at Cape Town etc.

At present Visiting Professor at Goethe University of Frankfurt, Germany and Raja Ramanna Fellow of Department of Atomic Energy.

First published short story in Vaigyanik, 1981 (in Hindi). Later about 10 short stories, about 50 poems, a novelette and several essays published or broadcast in Hindi. One Hindi short story made into a radio-drama by All India Radio.

Roots (1998) was the first story to be published in English. Most of the short stories have appeared either in the literary section or in the Festival issue of The Statesman.

The stories chronicle the rapid changes in the rural India and also the agonies and loneliness of people displaced from their roots, for whom their memories are like a shrine. The narrations are mostly in first person and recreate the atmosphere of a village fire-place or a bar.

Some of the stories have an undercurrent of exploitation of our villagers- every kind of it- by the rich and powerful as well as the calm composure and the acceptance of their fate as their dreams shatter.

Dedicated to

My Grandparents
Mr. Anant Lal Srivastava
& Mrs. Radha Devi Srivastava

&

My Parents
Mr. Ayodhya Prasad Srivastava
& Mrs. Prema Devi Srivastava 'Kishori'

&

My Grandchildren
Shaurya Joshi & Maya Joshi

Preface

"Ich bin ein clown; ich sammle augenblicke"

-Heinrich Boll

I try to live a life in my writings which I wish I could have. All the stories described in the following pages describe events as they were or as they should have been in my reveries. While they are acts of imagination it will be wrong to say that such people did not live.

My friends always tell me that I love to talk about myself. As a final act of 'revenge' on their 'unkind' remark I have put most of the stories in first person. This is also to felicitate my friend Heinigerd Rebel, who always laughed, when I told him something-the laughter starting from the bottom of his belly and shaking him thoroughly-and remarked, "Tell me, why do such things always happen to you!"

On a more serious note, a first person narrative gives us a space for exploring ourselves and our place in the universe. It also has the vitality of a confession, which like the water from The Ganges has the power to cleanse us of our sins, for a confession is also an act of atonement.

I have sat in bars and cafes of Europe, Americas, Africa, Bombay, Delhi and Calcutta, on the beaches of the Pacific, the Atlantic, the Indian Ocean, Arabian sea and the Bay of Bengal, and on hills over-looking forests covered with snow in the Himalayas and in the Alps, and in our balcony overlooking the city of Calcutta, and told all who were polite enough to listen about my village, where my children and my wife have spent only a few hours as the house stands deserted after my grand-mother's death. Am I trying to fill that void? I do not know.

I know several people who grew-up in villages and have never been able to go back. Many of these stories reflect their sorrow at this and the fact that their early life is like a shrine to them which they visit whenever they are in pain. Will they ever belong anywhere?

My teacher Dr. N. K. Ganguly used to tell me that he could not even go back to his village which is in Bangladesh now. He was in Calcutta when the partition took place, his parents joined him there, never to go back. 'Sir, this is to tell you that we villagers are forever refugees, even if we live in our own country.' Alas, he is not with us now.

Being a scientist by profession, I used to feel embarrassed (ashamed?) about my sentimentality and about my liking for literature. Along with Dr. Ganguly, my other mentors Brajesh Jain, Zillur Rahman Khan, Helmut Satz, and Bikash Sinha exorcized me of that guilt and told me to feel good about it. And now I indulge in this act shamelessly.

When we moved to Calcutta, I came in contact with Shyam Shrestha of Vishwamitra. With a lot of hesitation I gave him some of my writings in Hindi and to my surprise he liked them and printed them.

When I wrote the first short story of this series 'Roots' in English, I did not know what to do with it. The English press of India is invariably identified with the urban middle class and I was sure that no one would be interested to read about some fellow who cries about grazing cattle. My friend Pathik Guha left it at The Statesman. I was pleasantly surprised to know that Michael Flannery was going to include it in the Festival Issue of The Statesman, 1998. Since then he has accepted almost all that I wrote.

I often send my short stories to my friends- Steffen Bass, Jean Cleymans, Sri Prakash Dimri, Nutan Gairola, Charles Gale, Berndt Muller, Madhusri Mukerji, Shardindu Mukerji, Santanu Pal, Lakshmi Pandey, Saurabh Pandey, Madhava Saxena, Tej Singh and Yogendra Pathak Viyogi, and students Rupa Chatterjee, Umme Jamil, and Munshi Golam Mustafa. They invariably say nice things as they are polite and perhaps to encourage me. In recent times I did post some early versions of some of these stories on the Facebook and was pleasantly surprised with encouraging comments from many friends, e.g., Vaidehi Ganeshan, Ashok Kumar Jain, Anupama Pathak, Ashok Rathi, Dipali Saxena, Archana Sharma, and others.

My first and best critics have been my children- Richa and Mehul, and son-in-law Suraj, who read these stories with patience and made valuable corrections. My wife Rekha provides the ambience for me to indulge in this greatly satisfying activity and provides me a company which makes it possible to write and work for long hours at my institute and at home. She normally reads my stories only after they are published! This collection is a tribute to their tolerance of a friend's follies, for they have kindly treated me as a friend since long.

I must add one clarification before closing. Some of the stories describe events which have mentions of spirits and ghosts. This does not mean that I believe in their existence. But as these stories are often from rural India, their mention is inevitable, as people do talk of them.

I am most grateful to Mr. Venus Kesari who readily agreed to publish this collection of short stories written over a period of almost twenty years.

The six month long, calm and hassle-free sojourn at Goethe University of Frankfurt, Germany starting with mid-October 2017 gave me an opportunity to collect these stories and prepare them for publication as a volume. I grateful to Dirk Rischke for his kind and generous hospitality during this period.

My grand-parents and parents sacrificed all that they had so that we may have a decent education. Our grand-children have moved to Australia with their parents. They are too young for serious reading. But one day they will be able read these stories and then perhaps they will understand the complex influences which shaped us. They have already brought immense bliss and laughter in our life.

With love and gratitude, I dedicate this to them.

Dr. Dinesh Srivastava
Camp: Frankfurt, January 2018

Residence|: C3/44, Kendriya Vihar
V. I. P. Road, Mondal Ganthi
Kolkata 700052 India

Contents

1. Roots - 13
2. The Swine-herd's Mother - 28
3. A Slice of Mango - 38
4. The Well - 48
5. Protected by a Curse - 58
6. The Wolf on the Bridge - 66
7. Song of the Lonely Doe - 76
8. Droit du Seigneur - 88
9. Lotus in the Land of Edelweiss - 99
10. The Scar - 104
11. Daughters - 111
12. Requital - 118
13. The Yellow Villa - 125
14. The New Silk Route - 135
15. In Search of a Poem - 140

1

Roots

My earliest memories of the river are of a flood. The entire village had assembled on the big mound and was looking at the river which was in full spate. The river would be hardly thirty feet wide during the summer and one could even wade across it at many points. But now, it was more than two miles across, flowing rapidly, large eddies all over, and it must have been several tens of feet deep in the middle. Uprooted trees, occasional thatched roofs, branches and carcasses of some wild animals were floating along. We could see large snakes wrapped around the branches struggling to keep their heads out of the muddy water.

And then we saw the dolphins. They came in several big schools, surfacing out of the water most majestically, diving playfully, and emerging several feet away. They were swimming with their bellies up, or on their sides, swimming rapidly one way or the other, chasing each other, and racing each other. And they, like all the other fish were going upstream. We called them 'soons' and they reminded us of our playful calfs.

And the people were happy, as the floods were expected to take away the sand and deposit rich soil in its wake. We would have a good crop. The sighting of the 'soons' was always a good omen.

The forest across the river was glistening in the sun which had emerged after several days during which the rains had lashed us.

Yes, the forest. We could see both the forest and the river from the roof of our house. My grandmother told us of the tigers and panthers and bears and deer which were shot to extinction by the sahibs in that forest. We still had neel gais, and wolves, and jackals, and foxes, and hyenas, and porcupines, and cobras, and pythons, and the spirits of men and women who dwelt there. When you saw an animal or a bird, you had to look carefully whether it was casting a shadow. If not, it was definitely one of the spirits roaming as an animal or a bird!

The spirits of men could be either pretas, or bhoots, or pehelwans. The pretas were always thirsty and would be pleased if you offered them water. We had to know their abodes and pass respectfully around that place. The bhoots were nasty and had to be dealt with by either reciting Hanuman Chalisa, the forty couplets in praise of Lord Hanuman, or by saying a prayer to Lord Shiva in the village temple. Pehelwans were different. They were spirits of wrestlers and lived on mahua or banyan trees. They would materialize and invite you to a bout of wrestling. If you refused they would not let you proceed. You were always expected to wear shoes with thick hob nails and to keep them on if you agreed to have a duel. As long as you had the shoes on they could not do you any harm. As we were rather poor and never had any shoes, we settled for the next best-we carried a nail or a piece of broken knife, anything of iron. We also got talismans or taabeej or a very small seal of Hanuman, made of fired clay and painted black. A hole ran through it and seven or nine or eleven strands of new black threads were passed through it, either on a Tuesday or on a Saturday. And we tied this seal on our right upper arm. Armed with this seal of Lord Hanuman, we went boldly into the forest with our cattle. I recall only a few occasions when our friends were possessed by the spirits; normally the village ojha took care of them. The spirits of women were churails, who drank your blood; but that is another story.

We were expected not to hurt the neel gais, even if they entered our fields, though we could make every possible noise. Our dogs would any way run after them if they crossed the river to come into our village. By the time I was big enough to take our cattle to the edge of the forest for grazing, no tigers or bears or panthers were left. Jackals would come out only by the evening, but we were not to worry about them. If we saw them we only had to shout as if we were calling our dogs to chase them. I recall that we screamed 'lui ha, lui ha' when we saw them. As far as I know this phrase does not mean anything in our tongue as we speak today. Its real meaning is lost in the mist of time. Wolves were a lot bolder and would come out even during the day, some-times. They mostly hunted in pairs and we had to take special care that our goats did not stray out of our sights. They would some-times come very close to us, before we noticed them and start yelling for our dogs. Yes, our dogs were the true guards, though if they were not many in number they would only bark at the wolves from a safe distance. Foxes were too small to cause us any worry, though it was a good omen if they crossed your way from right to left, especially in the morning.

And the forest was full of birds! Parrots, both with and without yellow rings on their necks, hundreds of peacocks-whose fallen feathers we collected to make fans and to keep snakes away, teetars, baters, neelkanthas, doves, wild pigeons, shyamas, mynas, sparrows, beaver birds, ababeels, and many others. Oh, the forest was a veritable orchestra when all these birds started their calls, when a snake or a wolf or a jungle cat was on the move. And there were the monkeys, both rhesus and the more majestic langurs. Funnily, they would completely ignore us, if we were in a large group, but almost always tried to scare us, if they found us alone. We sincerely believed that they would pick out all the lice from your hair, if they were be-friend-ed. My grandmother gave us soaked gram to be fed to them on Tuesdays and Saturdays. They were a lot more likely to cross the river and enter our village where people would give them some food, or where they could scare a child- making him drop his food, or to eat from our mangoes and mahua and peepal and banyans and even our crops.

Yes the trees. I did not know the names of all the trees in the forest. There was this huge banyan tree. We were told that if you climbed the topmost branch you could see the Ganges which was almost twenty miles to the south of our village, where my grandmother went every Purnima with other women of the village, on foot, for a holy dip, singing all along. But of-course as we were not expected to climb the banyan tree, what we did often was to tie two aerial roots to make a swing, and swing for hours while our cattle dozed in its shade. Looking closely we could see some owls who would be uncomfortable with our noise and bats hanging upside down.

Our favourite trees were ber, jamun, kaitha, gular (fig), and tamarind. Ah, the sweet and sour bers-especially the little ones (jharberries as we called them) were the ultimate of delicacy. Often we had to struggle a lot to get across the thorns which adorned these trees and also from neighbouring babool trees before we could reach them. Kaitha, both unripe and ripe, and tamarind were our other favourite. We picked ripe bels and our mother made sherbet. We ate mangoes only as long they were unripe and sour. The ripe mangoes were for girls! We would eat the unripe mangoes and hold the slippery kernel between the thumb and the index finger of our right hand, and chant-"Kernel, kernel please tell me-which way does my maternal uncle live!" and then gently squeeze our thumb against the kernel. It would fly out in some direction. Sometimes it was right and when it was not-the older children told us that our maternal uncle was not at home!!

Come spring and the forest would get into a festive mood, what with so many flowering trees like dhak and semal, and a large variety of creepers.

Imagine a full grown peacock in its magnificent plumage, alighting gently from a low-lying branch of a dhak tree in full bloom, its turquoise blue feathers glittering against the bright orange flowers of dhak. Imagine an army of parrots perched on a semal tree -and taking off -their green feathers in dreamy contrast with the red flowers. Imagine a peacock dancing majestically against a back drop of darkening clouds heralding rains. Imagine hundreds of sparrows taking a dust bath to tell God that there was no water left in the forest for them to clean themselves properly, and that He should send rains. And imagine a flock of birds, a few hundred strong, alighting on our fields to feast on grain and flying away in unison at the slightest sound. Imagine a huge mangoe tree laden with fruits, and a rising wind turning into an aandhi (storm), and mangoes raining all around you-first the ripe ones, then the semi-ripe ones, and finally the unripe ones.

Imagine walking on grass adorned with millions of dew drops glistening like diamonds on a winter morning, into an envelop of intoxicating aroma of mahua flowers spread like a giant carpet under the tree. And imagine a morning enlivened by a chorus of hundreds of peacocks. And imagine an evening resounding to sounds of bells tied around the necks of hundreds of cattle returning from the forest across the river, their bellies full, and their mood pleasant. And imagine a dusk lit up by millions of fire-flies. And imagine a night, its silence broken by the occasional baying of wolves, and a howling of jackals at regular intervals. And imagine a river, teeming with egrets, and storks, and king fishers, and cormorants, and thousands of migratory birds traveling thousands of miles to the warmth of our river.

And imagine groves of bamboos. We made our lathis as well as our flutes from them. And the forest had its own flute! There were always a large number of bumble bees in the forest. These bumble bees would drill holes in the bamboos. With the gentlest of the breeze, the bamboos would sway and we would hear most melodious and divine tunes! We would hear the 'flute', get startled and then laugh, realizing that no spirits were involved.

There were a variety of cacti and bushes of all kinds, and creepers to cover them. Sometimes our grandmother would ask us to bring leaves, or the bark, or the roots of certain trees, or bushes, or creepers to make some medicines. It was always an adventure to shake the bushes with our lathis to scare out the hares who had their burrows underneath. Once they were out, our dogs would run after them, mostly losing them in the thick growth. Well quite often, we also disturbed some snakes in this process. I was not aware of "Jungle Book" at that time, I read it years later while living in Germany and had actually no problem imagining that the description could easily have been that of our forest. You see as kids we kept to the edge of the forest, which was at one end of a much bigger forest. If our little forest was so rich, the "real thing" must have been much more magnificent. Well..

A narrow trail passed through the forest-it was a short cut to the neighbouring town. The proper road took almost five hours of walk, while the short-cut took only about two hours. There was a big market in the town and people walked long distances to be there on Tuesdays and Saturdays. We mostly kept near the trail with our cattle, and envied the grown-ups who could go to the town. On both sides of the trail, kaans (elephant grass) and reed grew. After the rains the elephant grass would blossom, and its white flowers told us that the festival of Dashehera was not far, when we would be taken to the fair in the neighbouring town. Our aunts told us to bring back bundles of elephant grass and reed. They would dry the grass and the leaves of the reed. Then they would colour the leaves and make little baskets, elegant and intricate, and somehow always smelling good.

Oh yes, the trail. It was a sheer adventure to walk on this trail, where any one, including a snake, could be hiding on either side in the high grass. People always walked in groups. My grandfather told us of Beraham Thief and Robber Man Singh, who often came to the forest. He also told us of the time when during the Mutiny, the army of English men had gone along the village burning it down completely and razing every house to the ground, and when people had taken shelter in the forest. The forest had saved them and had provided food and shelter. The thick growth had deterred the soldiers and even though they knew that the villagers could be in the forest, they had not dared enter it. Many years later many freedom fighters took shelter in the forest.

You see this is my problem. I was talking of the river

and then started talking about the forest, and before long I would start about the mutiny and civil disobedience and British Raj. No! No! No!. That will not be right. Let me come back to the river.

I was telling that the river would be swollen only during monsoons. After the monsoons the river would shrink to about thirty feet, and water would get clear, and you could see all the fish swimming in it. The point where we could wade across it, with the water reaching up to our waists, or chests, would often shift every monsoon, and so would the activity associated with the ghat, as we boastfully called these points.

And there would be miles and miles of fertile land after each monsoon. Almost everybody would walk to the river for a morning bath. My grand-father always took his bath there. He would walk up to the river with a clean dhoti and a small lota. While coming back he would bring a lota of water from the river for puja. One day we found a small fish in his lota and my mother, who was well versed in mythological stories, told us of the Matsyavatar-when Vishnu was incarnated as Fish and was trapped in the kamandal of Manu, who had similarly gone for a bath in some river. She also told us that our river was on the route which Lord Rama took when he went to forest, and then to Lanka. If someone could find the spot where he crossed the river, we could perhaps find a speck or two of the dust off His feet. That would surely grant us nirvana!

Later the women would go with huge baskets and cut grass, bring it to river, wash the grass and come back with baskets full of green grass for the milch cows and buffaloes. In between, they would bathe in the river, swimming, singing, and exchanging stories of love and hate, of poverty and happiness, of lovers and husbands, of mothers-in-law and sisters-in-law, of strategies and intrigues, of affairs and elopements.

The washer men of the village would load their donkeys with dirty clothes-soaked earlier in ash and rehu (alkaline soil) and go to the river. The dhobi-ghat was near a bend in the river, where water was deeper, which was guarded by a spirit! Even at the peak of summer, we would have plenty of water there. They would thrash the clothes on wooden planks and then wash them in the river-spreading it out to dry. I recall that the clothes thus washed had a persisting smell of freshness..

There were also some fishermen in the village, but over the years they had become cultivators. Still, they would often go to the river with their special nets. These nets were made of three thin and long bamboo sticks, joined in the middle and bent to make three arches, their legs equally spaced along the corners of a hexagon and a net was fastened at this end. When they saw a large fish come out of the deep water and go upstream they ran along the river, and trapped the fish under their net by jumping over it. The fish was eaten only by the fisher men of our village, in those days. Others were strictly forbidden to eat fish. The kids of the fishermen, who often joined us with their cattle in the forest, would sometimes catch fish by using their dhotis as a net. Some adventurous kids smoked bidi and carried a match box. The kids would start a fire, apply a paste of mud on the fish, and roast them. Then they would break-open the fired mud and eat the fish, with some salt and chilli. On one such occasion I joined them, the taste of that fish still lingers in my mouth, though my mother who was a strict vegetarian, gave me a thorough thrashing when she learnt of it. I remember the thrashing also, as it stopped me from other adventures like smoking a bidi, or catching a snake by its tail, or making a chariot(!) drawn by scorpions, or stealing honey from bees by starting a smoke near the bee-hives, or driving a mongoose to where there could be snakes to start a fight. We learned to swim in the river and we washed our cows-who did not like it and our buffaloes who enjoyed it thoroughly. And we applied a coat of black or red paint on their horns, made from lamp soot or ochre and mustard oil.

During summer, my father would rent a field in the river-bed. One could get water by digging just a few feet, for irrigation, or just lift it from the river. We would plant water-melons, musk-melons, cucumbers, summer pumpkins, and bitter gourd there. The creepers for pumpkins and the melons grew almost a feet or two every day, and would soon cover the entire field. One of our workers would make a little hut to guard the field from neel gais and the monkeys and the cattle and the kids. And he had to stay in the field across the river, within sight of the forest during the night! I remember one occasion when out of nowhere a herd of wild elephants had trudged along the river bed and seeing our field, had taken a little diversion to feast on melons. They also smelled cane sugar fields, where the cane had been planted only a month earlier, and had decided to have a little dessert. While some villagers had tried to chase them, I remember my grandmother saying prayers to Lord Ganesha and telling that the elephants had come after a very long time! In fact they never came back after that.

Unknown to us, many changes were taking place. We had always believed that the forest belonged to all of us. We came to know that the entire forest belonged to the big land-lord!

And then one by one many things happened over the years. Men started appearing who would trap the rhesus monkeys. They had taken permission from the big land-lord. They told us that they would teach them to perform tricks. But they were not catching babies! It was only much later that we heard that the monkeys were being sent to far away America where they did experiments on them.

Before this news came the farmers would some-times express happiness at the reduction in the number of monkeys. And after the news of the export of monkeys came, the same farmers went about with a feeling of guilt that they had wanted them gone. Somehow, the langurs did not like this excitement and slowly but surely migrated to some unknown place.

Then bird trappers started appearing. They trapped parrots and bulbuls. For catching parrots, they would apply some glue to the tip of a stick, which fitted on top of another stick, and so on, making it a really long and thin pole, with glue at the tip. They would stand under a tree which was full of parrots, and raise this pole stealthily, to apply the gum in between their wings and sides. The parrots could not fly away and would fall on the ground, often dead. If they lived, they were put in a cage, which would be soon full of screaming birds. They had taken permission from the land-lord they told us!

We all knew that bulbuls were fond of red chillies, and as kids we would often take red chillies, fresh from chilli plants and scatter them under the tree having bulbuls. The bulbuls would fly down, pecking at the chillies. As kids we never harmed them and they were rather friendly with us, and would often sit on our shoulders and hands. These bird trappers, put chillies on the low lying branches of some bushes, which were additionally covered with glue. The bulbuls were easily caught.

There was a dry well and many deep holes in the forest. Their side-walls were full of natural alcoves, which for years had served as nests for the wild pigeons. The trappers would wait till dusk, when all the pigeons were back from their flights. Then they would cover the mouth of the hole with a net. One of them descended into the hole with a ladder and caught all the pigeons. The process was repeated over several years and soon our forest was denuded of all pigeons.

And then some fellows came and took away hundreds of nests of the beaver birds from the babool trees, to be sold as decoration pieces in cities. And we just watched.

And one day some fellows came and climbed into trees. They carried long poles with pointed ends. They gave out mating calls of jackals and wolves. To our surprise, we saw them emerge from their hide-outs even though it was still day time and go under the trees only to be stabbed to death. And the men took away their skins leaving the carcass to vultures. We heard that sahibs and mem-sahibs in big cities wanted to have coats made of the skin. And these men had taken permission from the big land-lord!

And then came the char-coal makers. They cut down all the huge trees systematically, converted them into char-coal and carted it away. Within a few years no big trees were left. We were also surprised that none of the spirits in the forest protested, though we waited eagerly for them to strike. Did they desert us too?

There was still a huge number of bushes which had remained untouched over several thousand years. The game-plan of the land-lord was getting clear to us. He wanted to clear the forest and convert it into fields for farming. Well it was his land, you see. Yes, the bushes.

Then he had an ingenious idea. He decided to produce bricks and tiles for houses being built in the town. And that really took care of most of the bushes, which were used to fire the bricks.

Soon the whole forest vanished and the land-lord's men leveled the ground, breaking it into smaller fields. Hundreds of snakes were scared out of their holes and killed during this process. And all the peacocks went away some-where. And yes, a dirt road was made which replaced the trail to the nearby town. The elephant grass and the reeds were completely uprooted to make way for the dirt road.

The remaining wolves and jackals took shelter into ravines made by the river, the neel gais migrated further down the river where a cousin of our forest was still surviving. Occasionally they did stray in the village and we delighted in their sight and almost welcomed them.

The land-lord started growing maize and gram in the fields created out of the forest, as these required a minimum of effort and you were not even expected to irrigate the field for these crops.

The river itself underwent a slow but perceptible change. The monsoon floods did not deposit good soil any more, the topsoil of our fields in the terai was systematically eroded and within a few years it was replaced by sand, which is what the river had started depositing every year. The river bed started rising and river became thinner and thiner during successive summers.

Then we saw the unseen. Our river which had been flowing even during the peak of summer, since times immemorial, went dry. Well, there was still water in some of the deeper spots, but the water did not flow, it got stagnant. The water at the washer-men's ghat started stinking, and even the buffaloes would not drink it. We waited eagerly for the rains to take away the dirty water.

The monsoon came, there was flooding, and rapidly flowing eddies. But there were no trees, and no branches, and no wild animals, and no snakes on the floating branches. It was just deadly, muddy, lifeless water. And we waited eagerly for the dolphins. They did not come, in fact they never returned.

Monsoon was over, the floods were over, the terai was free from river again, but the fields were full of sand. When we ploughed the fields, the upturned chunks of mud soon dried up and started blowing like dust even in the gentlest of the breeze. We knew that nothing would grow there. The women would go with huge baskets to cut grass, and come back with half empty baskets, in a surly mood.

The river was no longer deep, the water would be hardly a foot deep at most of the places, taking away the fun of bathing and diving. My grandfather stopped going to the river for his baths and started bathing at the well, just reciting the mantra which recalled all the sacred rivers.

Summer arrived, the river bed went completely dry. Even the washer-men's ghat went dry. They started going to the village tank where water was stagnant, and when people complained of the smell from the clothes they started going to the big river about two miles away. And the hot winds of the summer were now laced with sand from the river-bed. And we could not plant melons in the summer, as we dug almost thirty feet and found no water.

Then came the first reports of wolves attacking children. In earlier days, the most daring wolves would snatch a goat kid from a herd, but that was all. They never came into the village. I suppose that they had nowhere to go and nothing to eat. We had grown listening to stories of wolves bringing up lost or abandoned babies by suckling them and were completely baffed by this turn of events.

Around this time my father moved to the big city to the south.

Many years passed. I grew up, had my education, and with every “success”, kept moving further and further away from my village. Funnily, I often dreamt of my village and I always saw it complete with the river and the forest and the birds.

I now live in Calcutta, in a high rise building. I often tell my children of my early experiences with the river and the forest. I don't think that they believe me, but they are still polite.

Last year I went to my village with my son. My grandparents died quite some time ago, my parents live in the big city to the south of our village, and a lock hangs on our door. I still went, as the image of our ancestral house always haunts me in my dreams.

It was just after the winter but the river bed was already getting dry. I could only point to my son, the general direction where the forest used to be when I was a kid. Some measly crop of gram was growing there.

I could not gather courage to see all that had happened. I wanted to run away from there, before the happy images of my childhood village could be shattered completely and forever, leaving me without my roots.

We returned by a bus. Our river changes its course fairly frequently, and the road to the city to the south crosses the river five to six times within a distance of some twenty miles. And we keep moving towards the source of the river, which lies in a little lake further south.

Suddenly my son shouted, “Papa! Look!!”

There on the bank of the river among low cut elephant grass and reeds stood a pair of neel gais, majestic in their glory, their bluish necks glistening in the afternoon sun.

“I believe the stories of your childhood”, is all that he said.

And that is enough.

2

The Swine-herd's Mother

My village does not have much of a history. There are no ruins of ancient temples, or a fort, or a mosque, or even a dargah. The oldest 'objects' in my village were the peepal tree and the swine-herd's mother. The peepal tree could be seen from almost two miles, towering above the entire village and offering a divine protection to the entire village. Generations of villagers who made a pilgrimage to the shrines of Badrinath, Kedarnath, and Amarnath had brought rounded stones from the Himalayas, which were piled near its trunk and which were worshiped as Lord Shiva. My grandmother always proudly showed the holiest of the stones which our great-grand father had brought from the banks of Lake Mansarovar. He had also planted the peepal tree.

The swine-herd's mother, for that was her name, was thin as a reed, and black as a koel. No one knew her real age nor her real name. She was the village mid-wife, and there was no one in the village whose birth was not supervised by her. When not doing her job as a mid-wife she would go around the village with her herd of swine.

The swine foraged through the garbage dumps grunting and rolling in the drains, while the villagers booked the unborn piglets for sacrificing to Goddess Kali. Her piglets were widely famed to please the Goddess. The swine were resented and yet tolerated as the bearers of the offerings to the Goddess. She was also a living historian of the village.

As children we kept close to her-well as close as we could get without touching her and being "polluted" by her touch. If she were in a good mood, she could tell us the stories of the braveries of the village youth. She had every reason to be proud-were they not brought to this world with her assistance? Yes, there was always a ready band of young men in the village, who went around in a group, and who practiced in the village gymnasium, and who were the first ones to be out with lathis, whenever there was an attack of robbers, or elephants, or thieves, or sickness, or floods, or a snake bite, or a scorpion sting. They were the first ones to assemble and organize help when there was an accident, or a wedding, or an engagement, or a village gathering, or an occasion like Holi, or Shiva Ratri, or Ram Lila. And they were the first ones to ensure that no one got addicted to marijuana or alcohol. They were also the first ones to object when there was an oppression, any kind of oppression. She told us very proudly that 'her brave-boys' would not let any greedy farmer use his calves for ploughing the fields till they were fully matured. This, we knew, meant that the calves should have shed at least two of their milk-teeth.

As these young men married and settled down, they were replaced by their younger brethren. And the band continued to flourish. It was our defense against trouble, any trouble. And the entire village depended on them.

The swine-herd's mother, did not like the only other thing around the village which was older than her-the railways. Even though, she herself was untouchable, she was sure that people got "polluted" once they traveled by train and "lost their caste". But what could she do? Her own mother-in-law had told her that the railway line was built by Queen Victoria, who lived beyond the seven seas, and one had to obey the Queen.

But she could not reconcile with the thought that the railways also brought all that was unholy and unclean in the village. The railways took away so many village youths to far away Bombay, or Calcutta, and in olden times as far away as Rangoon which according to the swine-herd's mother was beyond the black waters well beyond Calcutta. They returned after several months and often years. And they brought disease and bad habits with them. And they gave their disease to their wives, who passed it on to the children. And as a mid-wife, she was the first one to know that one more family was affected by the dreaded disease for which she did not have any cure. But she was helpless, how else could one repay the debts of the village trader and the big land-lord? Fate, you see, is not easy to alter.

Oh yes, she still remembered the days when red-faced white sahibs patrolled the railway line on trolleys, inspecting the tracks and the bridge on the river and the culvert on the nallah. She also told us that the little railway station was always there. She might as well be right. You see my, village is on the track which goes from Calcutta to Amritsar. Just fifty years ago it went all the way up to Lahore. The Punjab Mail does not stop there. But the Punjab Mail is the most important train to pass through the station. For more than hundred years it has served as the clock of the village, as reliable as the Sun and the Moon and the Venus and the Great Bear. The train coming from Calcutta passes our village around noon and it is a signal for the workers in the fields to have a lunch break.

The train to Calcutta passes through the village around six in the evening, and signals the end of the day for the workers. And the swine-herd's mother could always be seen bowing to the train going east to Calcutta where her beloved Goddess Kali had Her abode.

But the Punjab Mail was not one of us. Our darling was the passenger train which came from Benares to go to Lucknow in the morning, and which went in the opposite direction in the evening. She was our link to the big city to the west of our village. Our people used it to go to the city for courts, and police station, and colleges, and hospitals, and markets, and to catch the Punjab Mail. It was also very convenient. It was supposed to arrive in the morning at ten minutes after eight. It normally came around nine thirty. And that was very useful. Our college started at ten. We were rarely late. The work in almost all the offices in the city picked up only by ten thirty. Reaching earlier was bound to be useless for our elders. In the evening it was supposed to start from the city at half past four. It rarely left the station before six which made it really very popular.

And like the swine-herd's mother, this passenger train was a living historian. She was witness to all the changes in the village. So, it had seen that the sons of the rich farmers had started going to college, after their schooling in the village junior high school. And it saw their attires slowly change from dhoti-kurta, to kurta-pajama, to shirt-pant. And she listened as the discussions of the village youth taking the train changed from Mahatma Gandhi and Swaraj, to Independence and elections, to education and jobs, to films and eve-teasing and frustrations over the years. The swine-herd's mother used to compare the railways to Mother Earth, who cared for all, fed all, and carried all, irrespective of their being good or bad! And yet, she did not like it, and was convinced that it would ruin our village completely.

So it was with a great deal of excitement that I started using this train when I joined the college. It was my first contact with the outside world. The students like me, who went to the city college would reach the station around nine and start their wait for the train.

And during this time, we would hear the news of all the neighbouring villages. From the “professional witness” we heard the latest on the property disputes and the criminal cases. When he was in good mood he would tell us of the finer points of law and tell us of his failures in winning the cases for his clients. The compounder in the civil hospital told us of the affairs of the nurses and the doctors, and of the attempted abortions by unwed mothers, and of the stabbing wounds which the goondas of the city Shahid and Maangeram had inflicted on their victims. And if prodded, he could tell that had they stabbed only one inch to the left or to the right or above or below, the victim would not have lived to tell his tale. In any case the “professional witness” told us that he had already been “hired” to tell that he had met the goondas in the holy city of Allahabad forty kilometers away on the bank of Ganges, when the stabbing took place.

The situation at the other end of the journey was somewhat different. It was a relatively big station and a junction at that. There were three big and pucca platforms, covered from one end to the other. And the railway station with its multitude of passengers and several trains, which came and went while we waited for our passenger train in the evenings, was to us what Gorky would have called 'My Universities'.

So we would see weeping girls go to their in-laws with anxiety in their hearts. And we would see parents sending their sons to faraway places for a job. And we would see mothers receiving their daughters-searching their faces for a sign of happiness.

And we saw the trains which brought hordes of Tibetan refugees. I also remember the long trains which passed through the station with men from the army traveling east to NEFA. We talked to the sober looking men in uniform, who were traveling to near certain death. We also collected contributions in the city and bought sweets and tea for them, and stood on the platform, shouting slogans, denouncing the enemies of our motherland. And I remember the long trains coming from the east with wounded jawans and officers without hands, or legs, but with a proud smile on their faces, marked with pain.

I should also tell you of the two restaurants on the station, one vegetarian and the other non-vegetarian. They had a common kitchen, though. The owner was always looking for young boys who may have run away from their homes and were caught by the ticket examiners. It was only much later that we came to know that the ticket examiners caught such boys and handed them over to the restaurant owner for a fee. There they were, working for a very small salary, and in return for food left by the passengers in their plates. As we were going there daily, we recognized all the boys, and saw them running with trays of food, cleaning the dishes and eating the food left by the passengers in the plates.

The newest leader of our band was the son of the big farmer in the village. He was the only child of his parents and always had some cash in his pockets. The pocket also contained a dagger which was only barely concealed. And there is a tale about his elevation to the position of a leader of the band.

I have already told that the passenger train used to arrive at our village station in the morning only by nine thirty. We recognized all the drivers and all the guards. In several years of my using the train, it arrived at the village station in time in the morning only once. And that day, every one missed it. It was quite clear that there was a new guard on duty who wanted to run it in time. So the next day we arrived at the station in time. The son of the big farmer met the driver and the guard of the train and asked them to co-operate, while we waited just nearby. The reluctance of the guard, who had started duty on this train only recently, was silenced once he saw the deliberately ill-concealed dagger in the deep pocket of our friend's coat and the rest of us. And we returned to our days of leisure and comfort. The son of the big farmer became our leader.

He confirmed our allegiance by buying us tea and samosas and betels and even cigarettes. And on such occasions when he was in a really good mood he could even buy us such forbidden things as omelets and toasts, and even a cold drink. We would normally arrive on the bench in front of the restaurants in the evening. He would immediately start ordering the boys who worked there. As it was also the time when three important trains arrived, the owner had to strike a very delicate balance of neither annoying us nor losing his other clientele.

The boys who worked there had to keep running to serve us, while we sat and laughed at his jokes, and at his comments on the girls who passed by, and at his stories about the harassments meted out to the teachers, and at his success in ragging the younger students, and at his tricks at cheating in the examinations. One of the boys had started saving his salary to be able to buy a ticket to return home. Perhaps an occasional thrashing by his step-mother was less painful than eating the left-overs and the bone breaking labour beginning with lighting the oven at four in the morning to massaging the legs of the owner and the waiters late in the night. So this boy dreamt of escaping one day. But the owner had other ideas

One day when we were having fun, we saw this boy sitting by the tap cleaning the soiled utensils. The owner looked at one of the waiters, and signaled. The waiter picked up several soiled plates and brought them to the boy. The boy turned to look and there was this big sound of breaking crockery. A few cups, and plates were broken. The owner started shouting at the boy and told him to pay up then and there. The price demanded was several times the cost of the crockery, but it also ensured that the boy could not leave for a few more months. The boy just wept and wept and wept. We looked at the leader, hoping that he would say something. He kept quiet. Later we saw the owner call the waiter and give him a five rupee note.

The following day was a Sunday. His father decided that their calf was now old enough to be put to work, even though it had not lost any of its milk-teeth. The swine-herd's mother was passing by, and she objected to this oppression, and expressed the hope that the band of young men of the village would never permit this torture. The young men assembled to see what was happening, saw the son of the big farmer himself supervising the yoking of the unwilling calf. And all the free tea and the samosas and the betels and the cigarettes put a seal on their lips. They went home, leaving the swine-herd's mother grieving and sad and dejected. Soon we forgot the unsavoury incident. A few days later the son of the big farmer acquired a pistol, to replace his dagger. Wc forgot all about the suffering calf and the boy in the restaurant and got busy with admiring his courage!

There was this pheriwala on the railway station in the city. He normally sold bananas. During winter he sold guavas and if nothing else was available he sold beads and combs and plastic fans. His calls were always very exotic and he sang out his wares in a clear sing-song style which was enough to quieten any wailing child. We advised him to get a helper who could carry his basket and then he would be free to serve more passengers. And one day we found that he had acquired a helper. The helper was just a boy, not much older than ten or twelve years. We assumed that the ticket examiners must have arranged that. The boy ran around with the heavy basket on his head and the pheriwala did brisk business. We never enquired about the salary of the boy, it was not our business.

But we were to know it soon. One day the pheriwala brought cucumbers. The boy was carrying the basket on his head, and the master was giving sing-song calls. It was hot. The peeled cucumbers dripping wet were a welcome relief. It was then that we realized that the salary of the boy was just the peelings of the cucumbers! After every round the seller would give the boy a few strips of the peelings which the boy wolfed down hungrily, smacking his lips. The seller had already made three rounds, but the train was going to be further delayed. The heat was unbearable. The boy had received only three helpings. There was a huge pile of peelings in the basket. The seller saw the boy eyeing the peelings hungrily and saw all the passengers trying to get his attention.

It did not take him long to decide. He emptied the peelings in the drain below the train and shouted at the boy to start working. I felt like screaming. The big farmer's son also saw this, looked at me and laughed. The whole gang of boys laughed with him. I knew that the village band would never again rise against oppression.

The festival of Navaratri was approaching. The villagers were waiting for the pig-lets to be born and were being assured by the swine-herd's mother that they would be ready on the appointed day. Her sows were roaming the village heavy with babies, grunting and the people would occasionally feed them. And thus it came to pass that one of the sows sauntered to feed on the mahua flowers which the big farmer had spread under the peepal tree for drying. The big farmer's son saw it, and shouted at the swine-herd's mother to take the sow away. The sow was already gulping the mahua flowers and was not paying any heed to her prodding. The big farmer's son shouted again, and took out his pistol. The swine-herd's mother pleaded not to shoot as the sow was carrying pig-lets for sacrifice. She also pleaded that the sow should not be hurt under the peepal tree which was so holy. The son shouted back that he did not care, aimed and fired. The swine-herd's mother stepped in, screamed in pain, and fell. The sow fled.

As if all this was not enough, some one noticed that blood from her wounds had spluttered on to the trunk of the peepal tree. A closer scrutiny revealed a drop or two polluting even the holy stones from the Himalayas. The big farmer's son immediately sold the peepal tree to a charcoal maker, who carted it away within a day.

The swine-herd's mother survived to supervise the birth of the pig-lets and their sale to the villagers who had placed orders with her. The day they were sacrificed to protect the devotees, she died. It was late evening, and she lived to see the Punjab Mail go to Calcutta to her beloved Goddess Kali and the return of the boisterous college going boys by the passenger train, for one last time.

Before her death she told her daughter-in-law, who was now her apprentice, that she should promise to sacrifice two pig-lets if she ever encountered difficulty while supervising a child birth. You see, she had sacrificed five piglets to Mother Kali, when the big farmer's son was born in a very complicated delivery.

And yes, my grand-mother collected the stone from the Lake Mansarovar and brought it home, even though it was no longer considered to be holy. That is all that remains of our past..

3

A Slice of Mango

Our house is in the middle of a mango orchard. My great-grand father who planned this orchard was fond of variety. And he planted a large variety of other trees as well, like neem, amla, jamun, ber, and mahua etc., in addition to mangoes. And he did not go for the kalami (grafted) plants. He opted for the deshi mangoes, grown from the seeds of ripe deshi mangoes.

This gave a very distinct character to each tree. They were all different. Their leaves were different, their fruits were different, their tastes were different, and they all looked different and even smelled different. And they all had a name! The names denoted some particular quality of the fruit or the tree. Thus we had a tree called Kathalia (The Jack-Fruit!) as its mangoes were rather big in size and when ripe, emanated a smell which reminded us of ripe jack-fruits. We shall hear more of it, later. And we had a tree called Hathi as its fruits could-by a slight stretch of imagination-be thought to resemble an elephant. And we had a tree called Cowrie-as its fruits were quite small.

And some-times the names alluded to some history. So we had a tree called Gandhi under which Mahatma Gandhi had rested one day a long time ago, and around whose trunk we had a raised platform of mud, which was often the seat of the village-council. One of the mango trees was just called Pagdandi (Foot-Trail) as it was close to where a trail passed several decades ago, when our village was taking shape. Now we have a pucca road there, but the name persists.

You see our life revolved around the orchard and every tree was like a member of our family. My grand-father and father continued with the tree-planting. Soon we were running out of names. My grand-mother used her prerogative to name some of them in various ways. Well! These names ensured that we all always knew the history of each and every tree. This was also very handy. So we could just go and play under the Kathalia, or tie our cow to the Hathi, or bring fire-wood from the Gandhi!

Where should I start? Should I start with the rainy season, when their leaves glistened-emerald green-when the sun was shining, and when we put swings on their branches where the young girls and the young brides of our village sang kajari till late night, and when the men sang Alha and wrestled in the akhara (gymnasium), and the kids played a game of 'rivers and canals' by joining the puddles and putting tiny boats in them with 'ants' to ferry them!

Let me begin from winter; it is just a convenient camp on the journey of seasons. As winter approached, the kharif crops which were mostly jwar, bajra, sesame, and urad would be home. Our workers would cut the stalks of jwar and bajra, their women would cut the ears having grain and the stalks would be stacked in bundles around the trees. These would serve as fodder for our cattle and a warm hiding place for children playing hide and seek. The family of our dogs used them to raise their pups for the warmth it offered. In any case once the pups were born we would make beds of hay for them, in a corner of our house, against the wishes of our mother as well as their 'mother'!

Come winter and the leaves of the trees would first turn yellow and then start falling. Their smell would pervade the entire orchard, which would be covered with a multi-coloured carpet of leaves, varying in colour from green to yellow to red-brick. You see, in general deshi mangoes yield a bumper crop every alternate year. During the year they do not yield a bumper crop, they shed leaves, and get new leaves during spring. We collected the dry leaves in huge bags and brought them home, some to be spread under the cattle, for warmth and for converting it to manure and the rest to be stored near the fire place.

During evening, we would start a fire, put some potatoes and sweet potatoes in it and assemble around it. As we ate the roast potatoes with salt and green chillies, my mother read from Ramayan, or told us stories from Mahabharat. Often our grandmother told us stories-tales of her own childhood, of our father and uncles, of our village and its spirits, of floods and droughts, of robberies and thefts, of courage and despair, of journeys and travails, drawing from her immense wisdom and experience. And she told us folk-tales.

The one we liked most was about the adventures of the seven sons of the King, one of whom was a mongoose! 'There was a King, who had seven Queens, but he had no sons. One day a holy man came. He told the King to pluck seven mangoes from a single bunch and give one each to his Queens. The youngest Queen was late in eating her share and a mongoose ate part of the mango she got. Well in due course of time, six of the Queens gave birth to sons, while she gave birth to a mongoose....' We had heard the story several times but one of the kids was sure to ask for it and she would tell it all over again.

The stories would continue till mother was ready with thick chapatis of bajra and a curry of new potatoes and urad dal with a lot of ghee and saag of either mustard or bathua, and of-course two or three types of mango-pickles!

By the time the festival of Shivaratri approached, the mango trees would be full of blossoms. The smell of mango flowers is very intoxicating; so much so that in our dialect of Hindi, the word for flowering of mangoes is same as that for getting intoxicated! The flower of mangoes is one of the most important items of the offerings to be made to Lord Shiva during Shivaratri. This had a very important consequence. We could pluck leaves of mangoes but only for a use in a worship or for decorating our house on festivals or marriages. No one ever cut a mango tree, not even a branch!. Its wood could be used only if the tree fell, though we did break the dried branches for use as fire-wood.

Within a month after this, the trees would be full of little green mangoes. They would grow bigger in size rapidly and the seed-coat of the raw-mangoes would start getting harder and that is the time when we plucked them for making khatai. For doing this we peeled off the skin, sliced the mangoes, removed the cotyledon and spread them out on the roof to dry, day-after day, till they shriveled. When they were free from all moisture my mother added spices and mustard-oil and put them in earthen pitchers, used for keeping pickles years after years. These pitchers would then be put in the sun to undergo seasoning. She would also put these in vinegar made from sugar-cane juice, along with garlic, chilli, cumin seeds, and jack-fruit.

In summer, we would play for hours and hours under them. People would often come and ask for a few raw mangoes to be added to the dal. You could choose a taste and a flavour and use mangoes accordingly. And we did not use knives for peeling raw mangoes, the acid in the mango acts on the knife and you get an odd metallic taste. We would go to the river and bring mollusk shells. And we would rub the convex side on a stone, till a large hole appeared on it. The edges of this hole would be sharp as any knife. We held these mollusk-knives in our palms and peeled the skins off the mangoes. And we sliced the raw mangoes and simply ate them with some salt and chilli powder. And we added some leaves of mint, salt, green chillies and gur (jaggery) to make chatney; every day a different chatney-smelling different, tasting different, to be eaten with meals and with sattu.

Soon the seed-coats of the raw mangoes would get very firm. Then we plucked the sweet mangoes and peeled them and boiled them in water. We added gur to them and ate them for snacks though in all fairness they made a very filling meal. And by the time, loo-the dehydrating wind of North-Indian plains started blowing, my mother would prepare panaa-a drink from either roasted or boiled mangoes-to be offered to anyone who came to our house and which was the surest guard against sun-strokes. And yes, I must add that the kernels of these boiled mangoes were kept in a corner of the court-yard, to get seasoned till the rains came, when we removed the seed-coats and ate the cotyledon! A powder of this could also be used with flour to prepare very special chapatis. And I must also add that while the rich farmers ate it as a novelty, for the poorer sections of the village this was the staple diet during the lean monsoon months, when there was no work for them.

Our orchard was also traditionally used by the entire village for the processing of the rabi harvest. This has remained the happiest occasion in a village from the times immemorial. For then, you had the fragrance of dried wheat and barley stalks, stacked high, and of mustard, and arhar and peas and gram. And you had the songs of the farmers as they took their bullocks round and round on hay spread in a circle to make chaff and used the gentle breeze to separate chaff from the grain. It was always a hard work and yet the sight of growing mounds of grain brought a ready smile to their faces. A chapati of freshly ground wheat and mango-chatney eaten in a mango orchard swaying to the call of koel is all that I ask for as my last wish!

The glorious times for the orchard was just before the mangoes started ripening, when the most expert climber of the mango-trees, Budhiram was called. He would come, make an offering of water and flowers and cloves to the spirits of the orchard, and reverentially climb the trees. He carefully plucked mangoes which would be caught in a net attached to a long pole. The house would suddenly be full of smells of spices-cumin seeds and coriander and turmeric and dry-red chillies and what not. The amount of spices used was so much that our stone grinding mill as well as the big mortar and pestle were used to prepare them. And the oil-man of the village brought freshly crushed mustard oil. At the end of it all, there would be dozens of earthen pitchers full of mango pickles, a large variety of mango pickles, lined on the roof and in the court-yard to be seasoned in the hot sun.

Most of the marriages in the village were also held during summer and our orchard was always used by the entire village as a camp for the marriage parties. During those days, it was common for the upper caste Hindus to bring along one or two dancing girls along with the marriage party. There would be a good mehfil (gathering) during the evenings, going till late nights. On such occasions white sheets would be spread on carpets under the mango trees, and people would sit around watching the girls sing and dance to the accompaniment of tabla, saarangi, and harmonium. The smell of ripening mangoes mingled with the rose-water which was sprinkled by the servants on the gathering and the connoisseurs of good music would request the girls to sing a composition in raag Basant or Yaman or Jaijaivanti, enjoying their renderings, their eyes closed, their heads shaking in approval. By the time we were ten years old, my grand-mother started sending us to attend these gatherings to learn manners of a mehfil and to get a feel for good music!

There would be male dancers with other marriage parties, wearing dresses covered with bells and dancing to the tune of drums and flutes, and singing a large variety of folk-songs, like Biraha, Kaherawa, Chaiti and Kabir. Well, well, well, our orchard saw all, listened to all and gave shelter to all.

Around this time we would find that the flesh of the raw mangoes had started turning yellow and the distinctly sour taste was giving way to sweet. Occasionally the crows would peck at one of the fruits to test them and they would drop. This was a sign that a time had come to pluck mangoes for ripening. Budhiram was called again, and he again climbed the trees and plucked the mangoes. We put them in huge baskets lined with leaves of a particular bush called roos or with hay and sealed the baskets with more leaves and mud. Within days the smell of ripe mangoes filled our house and before long we would be taking out huge quantities of mangoes, glistening like gold and smelling heavenly.

We would keep them in buckets of water and eat for hours, till our face and hands and clothes were all covered with mango-juice. And we would squeeze the mango juice on a sheet of cloth to make aam papad. We also squeezed a bowl of mango juice, sprinkled some salt on it and ate chapatis with it.

Not all the mangoes were plucked and many would be left on the trees to ripen there. This was especially true of our sour mangoes, which would be quite sour before the rains and tasted extremely sweet once the rains started. One of our sour mango trees was near a pond. The pond would be full of rain-water during monsoons. One of the kids would climb the tree and shake the branches, the mangoes would rain down in the pond, and we would take dives to collect them. Somehow the mangoes collected thus tasted much better. Fruits of labour?

Now I must let you in, into some family history, before I proceed. My grand-father had another brother, who was rather quarrel-some and greedy. To avoid trouble, our fields had been partitioned several years earlier. However the mango orchard had remained un-divided. We have a custom of not selling mangoes so it did not matter. However, once in a while, there was trouble. I have already told you that deshi mangoes give bumper crops in alternate years.

The Kathalia was our best mango, its fruits were big, fleshy, slightly sour when raw, and excellent when ripe. They had no fibres and only a thin skin covered them. They were the most preferred mangoes for making pickles, and it was common for the people of the village to come and ask for a basketful of mangoes of Kathalia for preparing pickles. Even though the tree was huge, during the lean years its yield was rather low. During one such year the brother of my grand-father started a quarrel about the quantity of mangoes he wanted. Soon the quarrel took an ugly turn, many bitter words were exchanged. Before it could develop into a fight the village elders came and advised that the orchard be partitioned too.

Next day the trees were counted and a line was drawn dividing them into two lots. The brother of my grandfather wanted the lot which had the Kathalia tree, which we also wanted. Ultimately a draw of marked sticks was ordered and when he lost it in three consecutive draws he cursed his fate and gave up. From that day, the bitterness between the families increased-with taunts and abuses and curses exchanged on a daily basis. The bitterness trickled down to the kids as well and soon the kids of the neighbourhood were divided into two camps which indulged in fights, which were taken up by their mothers adding to the estrangement.

Well, soon it was time to pluck mangoes for ripening. Budhiram came and plucked the fruits from Kathalia, took his share-normally one fourth and went home. For years he had been selling his share of mangoes from Kathalia in the neighbouring market as they were quite famed. We had a market every Tuesday, and he went to the market with these golden yellow ripe mangoes. My uncle had also gone to the market. He saw his cousin brother purchasing the Kathalias from Budhiram. He came back home and gloated over the fact that 'those fellows' were now 'reduced' to buying Kathalia from a 'worker' in our fields!

Around this time my grandmother returned from the village temple and heard her son rant and rave and gloat. She called me and my elder brother, filled two baskets with the best pieces of the mangoes from the heap of ripe Kathalias and Hathis-the later famed for their fragrance. And she went with us to give them to her husband's brother, who had insulted us in every possible manner during the preceding month.

And I tell you, at that moment her eyes were

glistening with some unknown sparkle, somewhat like the sparkling white cotyledon of the raw mangoes when they are sliced.

Many years have passed since then. The Kathalia tree was uprooted in a severe storm some years ago. My grandmother is no more, but every year my mother sends some baskets of choicest mangoes to the house of my father's cousin.

I have in the meantime become a painter. I do occasionally paint women. And every time I paint the eyes of women, I paint them to look like a raw mango sliced into two. People have often accused me of copying a painter of Bengal but how do I explain to them that I am forever saluting the spirit of my grand-mother.

4

The Well

You could see our well, well before you entered our village. It was situated on one of the high grounds in the village, close to a huge mango tree on one side and a tall peepal tree nearby. In the morning you were sure to find one of the villagers bathing there, invoking all the holy rivers of India or drawing water to offer to Lord Shiva in the form of stones placed near the trunk of the peepal tree. In our tongue we call water as pani. However, if the water is to be used for a puja, we call it jal. I can recall many occasions when someone had called the water drawn from the well as pani and my grandmother had refused to use it for puja, or to offer it to Lord Shiva! No wonder that a lota of water from the well was often used as Ganga Jal by the villagers, especially in village councils, to take an oath.

When we were kids, the well was a place full of stories. We would assemble around the well, under the mango tree and just listen to the elders talk. The long lazy days of summer were ideal for this. During summer, when the sun was shining-or rather burning, most ferociously and loo-the dehydrating hot wind of our north Indian plains was blowing, you could see the old brahmin lady sitting under the mango tree with an earthen pitcher full of cool and refreshing water from the well to offer the travelers through the village.

Once in a while, you could see dust-devils forming, traveling some short distance, going around one of the trees, or around the well and exhausting themselves. Their sight always encouraged her to tell us of the glittering golden vessels full of gold coins and jewelry and diamonds and pearls, which came out of the well and sat on the rim of the well. According to her, many people had seen them, but when they had approached the well, the vessels had jumped back into the well. Some people had even seen the vessels glistening through the water when they peeped into the well, only to vanish soon afterwards. You see, spirits, buried treasures, and serpents with mani on their heads were the staple diet of our imagination.

It was at the well that we learnt about all the spirits which resided in the village. The most famous was the Dhamasa Devi, whose abode was just a few hundred meters away near the village tank. We were told to seek her blessings when we left our village for any work. She protected our village from plague and pox and cholera and theft and robbery and even locusts. She had been seen in various forms by various people. My uncle had seen her as a big bull, going around in a rage or while coming to drink water at the well where we always kept a trough, full of water. Some-one had seen her as a buffalo which changed into a camel which changed into an old lady and then again into a buffalo, before he realized that he was seeing the goddess. The moment he said the appropriate prayers and promised to light a lamp and offer five cloves at her abode, she had vanished. Some people even claimed to have seen her 'procession', complete with horses, elephants, palakis and musicians, proceed to the tank and vanish.

My grandmother always told us of the aunt of my grandfather who had committed sati, and whose chaura (place) was by the side of our house. Her presence gave our family an added aura. Married women of our village always brought their new sarees to her place as an offering, before using them. We always sought her blessings before embarking on a journey. She was also the guardian of our family. So much so that one thief had even asked for forgiveness from my grandfather after he had cut a saindh (hole) in the outer wall of our house and had seen the Sati Devi, towering over him. She was often seen going around the well and the mango tree, halting at some places, inspecting some changes-on full moon nights.

During the rainy season, you could see the villagers assembled, under the mango tree, around persons singing Alha, the ballad of the heroic deeds of the twelfth century heroes-Alha and Udal of Mahoba, their drums rousing the villagers, their songs wafting over the village. Ah the bravery of Alha and Udal-even the nature of Mahoba was full of bravery. The croaking of the frogs of Mahoba was enough to scare wild elephants! How can any one forget the women of Mahoba who prayed to dark clouds for heavy rains so that their husbands could spend just one night at home.

It looked as if the well had always been there and the scenes had remained unaltered over a long period of time. Throughout the year, travelers walking across the village would often rest a while near the well and chat about the - happenings in their own villages with any-one who happened to be around. They would talk about the crops and cows and bullocks and fairs and land taxes and court cases and robberies and snake-bites.

And they would talk about the boys in their community who had reached a marriageable age and about girls for whom suitable families had to be found. Child marriage was still common, especially among the backward castes, and it was rather common for fathers and uncles belonging to such communities to carry a lathi with marks indicating the height of their wards of marriageable age.

The talk of marriage reminds me of a very interesting custom at which the young girls of today would definitely frown. When a boy was getting married, and his marriage-party was ready to depart for the bride's place, his mother would go to the well. She would sit on the rim and start lamenting that her son was going to get a bride and he would soon forget her. She would then say that she planned to jump into the well and end her life! The bride-groom would then go to her and say, “Mother!, I am not going to get a bride, I am going to get a maid for you!!”. Having thus ensured her supremacy in the house, she would bless him!

We also learnt of the only major scandal of our village from one such gathering. Many decades earlier, the grand-father of our present village-chief had invited the officials of our district for a hunt. They came with their large retinue and the entire village was pressed into their service. The women of the village were asked to help with the cooking and cleaning. Dancing girls from the city had been called to entertain the visitors. A band of gypsies had also been called to provide additional entertainment. We learnt that four of the women of the village were so enamoured of the life which the peons of the sahibs led that they had eloped with them. Even though it was a rather old story, the villagers would often talk about those women in disparaging terms for having brought disgrace to the village.

The water from our well was very sweet. There were many other wells in the village but they all had somewhat brackish water. Most of them were also rather shallow, while ours was very deep. As kids we used to boast about the length of the rope needed to draw water from our well- it was a full sixty fathoms. The bottom of the well was definitely many more fathoms beyond this, and we believed that if you kept going you would reach Pataal Lok where King Bali ruled. It was lined with bricks and an ancient mortar. The mortar, we were told was made from a mixture of lime, sand, ocher, gum of acacia, bel and gur. There was a nice platform around the well. This pucca platform around the well was built by the grandfather of our village-chief as a gift to the village when he had won the large contract from the English rulers to supply food grains to the Indian Army during the Second World War.

The well had a diameter of more than ten feet, and on one side we had arrangements for drawing water for domestic use, while on the other three sides we had arrangements for pur, in which a pair of bullocks draw water, with the help of huge bags of leather. During the season of rabi crops we would often have six pairs of bullocks drawing water continuously. Our well was very popular and even such farmers who had fields fairly far away from our well were eager to irrigate crops from our well. They all knew that the crops were always much better, when they took water from our well. When not in use, the well-trodden inclined stretch of land around the well became our play-ground.

Even at the height of summer, the well would be busy. There were quite a few farmers who would plant sugar-cane or tobacco or vegetables. These would need to be watered during this heat. The only shade would be provided by the huge mango tree which covered the entire stretch of the paudar-the inclined stretch down which the bullocks walked while pulling the bags full of water, their masters walking behind them, urging them on.

No wonder that on the day of Diwali, every family would send an earthen lamp burning ghee at the well, as a mark of gratitude. You can easily imagine the beauty of the well, glittering in the flickering lamps on the moonless night. It looked as if the well was smiling.

Our well had the reputation of never going dry, not even when there was a severe drought. The inclined ground around it was the place, where we would start our agitation against the gods when there was no rain. All the young boys of the village would assemble near the village and sing in unison:

> "O Dark Clouds, give us rain,
> Else from stealing your Grandma,
> We would not refrain!"

At this the women from the village would pour water from the well on us, and we would roll in the mud, making a great show of our demand. After this we would go from door to door repeating the procedure. If this also did not work then the young men belonging to the upper castes would assemble near the well, lament about the bad times and then go around the village, 'begging' at the houses belonging to the lower castes. That was sure to soften the hearts of the gods!

The evenings at our well were always full of charm-rustic, raw, and full of laughter. Women from even far away houses came to draw water for cooking and drinking. It was always a pleasure to see so many young women flock to our well, many of them recently married and thus covering their face with the corner of their sarees. They came in groups, often singing, laughing, teasing each other; their glass bangles jingling, their paijebs (a silver ornament for ankles) producing music, pure and joyous. It was somewhat difficult to pass the village after Basant Panchami without being splashed by mud thrown by one of the women! Have you not heard the song; "Come Spring and mud in the hands of young women becomes sandal-wood paste!"

Often a merchant, called pathaer selling bindis and kohl and ribbons and talismans and beads and hair oils and hair-pins and threads, came with his wares and settled near the well. He knew that it will have a good gathering of the women of the village. Children and women would immediately surround him and watch him take his valuables out of his huge bundle and spread them out in front of him on a sheet of cloth. The women would get busy with the imitation jewelry and alta and sindoor.

Young mothers would ask him to make a kardhan (girdle)-a thin cord of several strands of black threads to be tied around the waist of young children. We delighted in this as it was always made to size. He would take the measurement and spread his leg out, running the shining black thread around his fore-finger and the toe of his feet. When the required number of strands were ready he would take the cord out, make a loop at one end and a little knot at the other. The best part was when he took out the shining golden thread to cover the knot. We would all exclaim, with joy, simple joy, delighting in its brilliance. He also sold taalismans against fevers and dysentery and bed-wetting and restless sleep and nightmares. And he carried the most exotic chotis, the multicoloured cords of thread to be woven into the hair of women. He knew all the women, of-course as the mother or the daughter-in-law or the daughter of so-and-so. He would often sell the goods on credit and come back to collect the costs after harvest.

And the woman selling glass bangles also came there often. She carried this huge basket full of glass bangles, glittering in the sun. The women would see the bangles and touch them and feel them and sigh with resignation if they were too expensive.

There is something very poetic about the jingle of glass bangles worn by young women, as their hands go up and down along the rope while drawing water from the well. I suspect that the women used to enjoy the sound thus produced and also the effect it used to have on the passers-by, who were sure to slow down while passing near the well. If you have not experienced this, you can never understand the rationale of Lord Krishna hanging around the panghats.

Our post-man never bothered to go from house to house, he would just come and settle near the well and read out the names of the recipients, someone or other from the family was bound to be there. If they were not, they would be called and soon there would be a good gathering near the well. He would often be asked to read the letters. It was customary for the writer to send greetings to a large number of people by name, and he would go on reading names, or the relationships, and the assembled people would shake their heads in happincss at being remembered. He would also bring the money-orders from young men working in places like Bombay, Calcutta, Ludhiana, and Delhi. Someone or other was sure to get him sherbet or just gur and fresh water from our well.

The wives of young men who were away surrounded the post-man to write letters for them, or just waited to hear the news from their husbands. While it was common for the young men to enquire about their mothers and children, it was very unmanly to enquire about their wives, and they never did so. The letters were for everybody to hear.

The brick-lined walls of the well were often damaging our brass and copper pitchers and buckets. Once in a while, a thathera came who repaired them. The snake charmers and the magicians and the men with monkeys and bears, all assembled around the well where there was always a ready audience, and where a gathering could be assembled very quickly.

So it was but natural that our present village-chief, the grand-son of the old land-lord who had built the platform around the well, came to the well to inform that a water-tank on a pillar was to be built in the village and pipe-lines would be laid-out to vantage points for taps. Several tube wells were bored to provide water for irrigation at various places in the fields.

The work was completed rapidly and the well was soon deserted. Grass started growing around the platform and a peepal started growing on the inner wall of the well. Some snakes started living in the rapidly growing vegetation. People forgot about the well and during the Diwali no one put lamps there. The impromptu assemblies around the well stopped. A few years later, the platform around the well cracked under the pressure from the roots of plants growing on and around it.

The crack revealed four skeletons. They belonged to women. They even had their glass bangles and paijebs on. The skulls of the women had been smashed. However any doubt about their identity was removed by the metallic emblem normally worn by the peons of important district officials on their belts, which was also found there. The entire village participated in performing their last rites.

After that day, once in a while on a full moon night, four women are seen-laughing and singing and jostling each other, and drawing water at the well, which somehow regains its glory on such occasions.

And ever since, the well has regained its place in the pantheon of the village.

5

Protected by a Curse

I have known Ramdeen for the last fifty years. He must be nearing eighty now, but not much has changed in his appearance over this period. He is just slightly, only very slightly, bent at the back, and yes his hair has turned snow-white. He still sports his flowing beard and his mustache is as luxurious as it was 50 years ago, when it was jet-black. And he still carries his hand-held spindle and a small bundle of snow-white hemp making thin, strong, and uniform strings of hemp, while walking, while talking, while sitting in council-in short all the time.

Ramdeen is the rope-maker of the village. His ancestors were famed for the quality of their ropes and supplied ropes to the army of the Nawabs and the Rajas of Awadh. Even now Ramdeen maintains that an elephant shackled with an iron chain feels 'imprisoned' while one tied to a rope feels, at the best, 'disciplined'! Well, the Kings are gone and so have the Nawabs. Now Ramdeen makes ropes and strings for all the needs of the villagers.

Hemp is widely grown in our part of the country. You sow hemp, after the first monsoon rains, ploughing the field just once. And you sow it very dense, so the plants grow very close. Hemp grows rapidly, soaking up the rains. In earlier days, when chemical fertlisers were not known, the farmers would often plough-in the plants when they were just about a foot tall; especially if they planned to grow wheat. Hemp also helps nitrogen-fixation in the soil and the farmers have used this simple method for centuries to increase the yield of food grains. By the end of the rainy season, the hemp plants grow to a height of about six feet and are harvested. By this time the 'bark' of the plants is quite fibrous. The top-portion of the plants is still tender and is chopped off as fodder for the cattle. The rest is tied into bundles having a diameter of about four-inches which can be held in hands.

Ramdeen used to buy these from the farmers. And then his back-breaking labours started. He would carry the bundles to the village pond and float them in the water. And he would load them with mud from the pond and stick a flag to mark the day when he put them there. You could see several such floats in the pond, with their colourful little flags fluttering in the wind. In a few days the hemp was ready. Ramdeen would go into the pond, choose the float and methodically take the little bundles of hemp and beat the water with them, swinging them overhead, and thus separating the fibers from the rotten skin of the hemp plant. After several such beatings, much like the flailing of clothes by the village washer-man, the shining white fibers emerged, and he stacked the bundles on the side for the water to drain. You see it requires great expertise and experience to get the best hemp. If he delayed-the fibers could get weak, and if he was too early-the rotting part of the bark would not separate from the fibers and discolour them and also reduce their strength and make them heavy.

You should also not forget that rotting hemp really stinks and standing in the pond for hours with this stinking smell all around and doing such a labourious job is quite exhausting. And since this activity has been going on in the village pond for several generations, the pond also shelters a large number of leeches. While Ramdeen would be struggling with the hemp they would feast on his legs and get bloated. Knowing fully well that they were feasting on his blood, he would continue to work and just casually remove them when he walked out. Within a few days his legs would be covered with festering wounds and I suppose that it was only his strong constitution that prevented further serious harm, year after year.

When the hemp was dry, he would very gently remove the bone-white sticks of the hemp plants which are used for making roofs of huts and 'demons' during the festival of Dussehra. And then he would start with making strings and ropes of the hemp. This cycle of rains and hemp-cultivation and rope-making has been going on for the last seventy years of his life, as by ten his father had trained him in every aspect of rope-making. And this back-breaking work has kept him in good health during all these years, though his great-grand-son does not permit him to get into the pond now.

During the Second World War, his friend Kanhaiya Lal bagged a large contract to supply ropes of various thicknesses to the Indian Army. He went around the villages buying hemp and encouraged Ramdeen to employ additional workers to make ropes. They toiled hard and together they made a tidy sum. Ramdeen started dreaming of building a decent house and buying some land.

However the gods who sent leeches to feast on him when he laboured had other designs. One day his cow somehow got entangled in a rope which he had spread out to dry and choked itself to death. He offered to perform atonement and give a feast which would consume about twenty-one seers (about twenty kilos) of salt. However the village council, under the pressure of the upper caste villagers-who had grown jealous of his prosperity, refused to accept the request. He was sentenced to lead the life of a beggar for one year and give the feast of atonement on his return. He was also to carry the tail of the cow as a symbol of the sin he had committed. This was designed so that he told the story of the cow's death where-ever he went, and so that he could not draw water from a well, as his touch was polluting, till he had lived-out the punishment meted out to him.

Ramdeen sold all his ropes, the unused hemp, and the remaining cattle. This along with his savings amounted to some twenty gold coins (asharafis). He deposited them with his friend Kanhaiya Lal, sent his wife to his in-laws, put a lock on his door, and with a glance on the hemp fields ready for harvesting went away to lead a beggar's life for one year. He traveled to Kashi, Prayag, Haridwar, Mathura, and anywhere where his fancy took him. He slept under trees, near temples, on ghats of rivers, and on the platform of wells. He lived out his atonement, begging for food and water and enduring every possible suffering, secure in the belief that his wife was safe with her parents and his wealth was safe with his friend. These journeys and hardships somehow turned him into a very calm and religious man, respectful of gods. He returned a year later and with some help from his in-laws gave the feast for atonement. He brought back his wife, who had delivered a son during this time.

It was again time to harvest the hemp and he went to Kanhaiya Lal for the gold coins so that he could start his life. To his utter dismay, Kanhaiya Lal refused to even acknowledge that Ramdeen has given him any money to keep. Ramdeen was completely stunned. But he had always been a man of few words. He just asked his friend to go to the river with him, stand in the water and repeat that he had not received any gold coins to keep. Ramdeen watched in further disbelief as his friend went through the motions of denying it under 'oath' in the name of Mother Ganges. Ramdeen only said, “Kanhaiya Lal, if I have never hurt any-one knowingly, may the leeches which feasted on my blood when I slaved for saving that money turn into snakes.”

It was evening. Ramdeen decided to borrow money from the money-lenders next day. He was a good worker, the market was still upbeat, and he was sure to secure a loan. However, the night was disturbed by screams from Kanhaiya Lal's house. His eldest son, who was just eighteen, died that night-of snake-bite. Kanhaiya Lal ran to Ramdeen's house to return the gold coins and ask for forgiveness.

Ramdeen only added, 'I hope that none of your descendants do such a thing, either'. Kanhaiya Lal took a promise from Ramdeen that he would not tell of the curse to anyone. He also asked Ramdeen to come to his house every day, so that he may never forget the curse.

Ramdeen kept his promise and paid a visit to Kanhaiya Lal every day. They sat facing each other, Kanhaiya Lal reading Ramayan and Ramdeen making strings and ropes. And that is how people remember them. But now I wonder about the continuous pain and remorse which must have tied the two friends together.

This did not last for long. Kanhaiya Lal took to bed within a few years and died. At the time of his death, he told his other surviving son, Shivaram about the curse and also of the promise he had taken from Ramdeen. Shivaram had studied Law at Allahabad and was becoming a fairly successful lawyer. Shivaram felt very uncomfortable at this demand but gave in to the pleadings of his dying father and promised never to lie under oath for any material gains. Ramdeen kept his promise too and kept coming to the house of Shivaram, every-day, as a reminder from Kanhaiya Lal, even though he definitely felt somewhat unwelcome.

However, in the heady days of youth, Shivaram soon forgot the curse and the promise he had made to his father on his death bed. After-all all his colleagues were doing such things without any mishap. He started toying with small lies to ride over inconvenient parts of the court-cases he was contesting.

Around this time a robber was caught in a neighbouring village. Shivaram pleaded the case of the robber in return for a hefty sum. He bullied many of the witnesses into giving contradictory replies. He further trained a perfect alibi who testified under oath of dining with the robber when he was alleged to be committing the robbery. The oath was taken in the city-court around two in the afternoon.

It was the rainy season. Shivaram's elder son, Govind, was playing with other children near the pond which was surrounded by mango trees full of ripening mangoes. Ripe mangoes were dropping into the pond and the children were diving to collect them. Govind took a dive and did not surface for long. Elders were called, and his body was recovered-a water snake had entangled his feet, causing him to drown.

Shivaram was young. Shivaram had good education. Shivaram was not superstitious. He himself had not taken the false oath, and decided that it was just a coincidence. He told no-one about it.

I am the third son of Shivaram. Govind, who had died

in the pond, was my eldest brother. My father had always told us that his second son-my elder brother-was lost in a stampede at a Mela at Allahabad, during early fifties. I had grown seeing my mother agonizing over the loss of her two sons. She would often talk of the second son being, perhaps taken away by some cruel persons or a gang of sadhus, or a gang of thieves.

We received a letter from my father asking me to go and see him. As we had visited him just a few months earlier and live faraway, I was surprised. He was quite ill and my mother and other villagers had assembled around him. Seeing me he asked others to leave, except for Ramdeen who continued to sit there spinning his spindle.

My father told me the following. It was true that he had gone to Allahabad, several years ago during one of the Melas, however it was to attend a court-case at the Allahabad High Court. He had taken along my brother, who was young and keen to see the city. He used to rent a suite in a hotel near the Civil-Lines. Once again he had 'trained an alibi' for a person who had committed a murder. His client had been acquitted and he had returned to his hotel to see his son sleeping in his room. He did not notice that the son was dead-of a snake bite, till he was ready to go out for a dinner. As he had taken the case against the advice contained in the promise to his father, and reinforced by the silent gaze of Ramdeen he returned home to tell that his son was lost in the stampede at the Mela.

I was born a few years later and was sent to live with my aunt in Calcutta, with explicit instructions to educate me to be a professor, which I am now. He continued with his profession, though he limited himself to training young lawyers, and doing things such as getting property searches, preparing wills, and writing well researched commentaries. And yes, he started welcoming Ramdeen to a regular reading of Ramayan, during evenings. I went home during vacations and saw them often sitting together, not knowing that they were tied together by pain and suffering.

I hope that I never let go of this image of my father, half reclining on a cot, and slowly and painfully whispering the details of the temptation, the tragedies and the cover-up; the silence being broken only by his breathing and the spinning of Ramdeen's spindle.

It will soon be my turn to pass on this message to my son. I only hope that he will believe me when I tell that while it may be all right for others to cheat or to lie under oath, we the descendants of Kanhaiya Lal are protected from this temptation by the curse of a rope-maker.

6

The Wolf on the Bridge

Mohan Lal worked for the railways till he retired. He joined the railways at a young age of twenty-one in the turbulent days of 1930s, as a gang man. The movement of Mahatma Gandhi against the British rule was picking up and people had started looking down upon government jobs. Mohan was practical, he had a family to feed and more than four acres of his prime land had been mortgaged with the village trader to raise money for his father's last rites. There were very few occasions in the past, when any-one mortgaging his lands with the trader had got them back. The interest rate was simply too high-it used to be called "takahi byaj" which meant an interest of two paise per rupee (a rupee used to have 64 paise those days) per month, compounded yearly. This came to an interest of almost forty percent.

Mohan Lal was very lucky that he got a job with the railways. Most of the villagers of his age group had to move to Calcutta to pull rickshaws or to work in jute-mills or to work as a domestic help at very low salaries. He often told us of the examination which he had to pass to get the job. He was asked to lift a huge teak-wood log which must have weighed much more than a hundred kilograms. He had summoned the help of all the gods he knew and with a single minded determination picked up the log and even walked several feet before dropping it. His eyes had bulged with effort, and only a thought of hardships which he was to endure, if he failed, had helped him hold on to the heavy weight, which was much heavier than he had expected it to be.

Only after dropping the log he had noticed that several steel rods were inserted in the log, and he came to know that the Inspector could have removed some of them in exchange for a few hundred rupees. He still had to pay a bribe of about five hundred rupees, which was a considerable sum those days, to get through the medical test-though there were not many in the neighbouring villages who could wrestle with him for more than a few minutes. He had sold two of his murra buffaloes and a pair of his famed nagauri bullocks to raise the money. It was only much later that he saved enough to buy a replacement for the cattle.

Gang men maintain the railway tracks. It is a monotonous and labourious job which has never been noticed by babus who travel by the highly subsidized passenger and express trains-often with-out tickets, and who indulge in denigrating anything that is Indian-it could be the Indian Railways, or the Indian political system, or the Indian education system. A rapidly moving train traversing the vast plains of northern India with farmers struggling with Nature to produce food for all, stirs their conscience and they indulge in the only intellectual activity they have ever known-to denigrate India. Well, when Mohan Lal joined the railways, he also had to listen to their abuses, for “selling his soul to the British”.

Oblivious to their sentiments, Mohan Lal worked on the tracks. It involved removing all the ballast using a pick-axe and a heavy rake, cleaning it of dust and accumulated garbage, and putting it back there, thus restoring its shock absorbing capacity. If the trains moved fast the stones were rapidly displaced from below the tracks and had to be rearranged more frequently, and more carefully. When it rained, Mohan Lal and his colleagues had to be extra careful to ensure that rain-water did not accumulate near the tracks and the track-bed did not get soft.

And it went on from winter to summer to rains to winter to summer to rains. And during this time, Mohan and his colleagues had only a simple food to eat, they brought some sattu or puffed rice and ate it during the drinks-interval, and made some bhauri to be eaten with roasted potatoes or brinjals, and green chillies and raw onions for lunch. For making bhauri, you mead flour and make a really thick chapati-almost one inch thick and having a diameter of about three inches or so. And then you bake it over a slow fire of dried cow-dung, for which there is never any scarcity in rural India. Mohan Lal and his colleagues would return home late in the evening tired and exhausted, and their wives would give them an oil massage to relieve them of the aching muscles, applying a bit of turmeric powder on any injuries that they might have received during the day. But Mohan Lal did not complain, he was able to pay off the interest on his field, his wife sold the milk from the remaining buffaloes and slowly they started living reasonably well.

It was almost ten years since he had joined the railways. By this time the movement for India's freedom had gathered considerable momentum, and there were students who took pride in destroying the railway tracks, almost always in isolated places, which added to the difficulties of men like Mohan. The inspector of tracks is known as a Permanent Way Inspector.

In those days one Mr. Wilson was the inspector for his section of the track. Mr. Wilson was waging a personal war against the movement of Gandhi, and in his view all Indians deserved to be put down 'into their bloody place'. He demanded complete obedience from his staff and he expected all the gang-men to lie prostrate to salute him when he came for inspection. Thus he was extremely annoyed that Mohan stood erect and only folded his hands to salute him when he came for inspection. Mr. Wilson was alone that day. He only shouted at all the gang-men for no reason at all, abused them thoroughly, and left on his trolley pushed by two workers. He returned a week later for an inspection, accompanied by two police-men. Again while the rest of the gang-men lay prostrate in front of him, Mohan just stood politely-with folded hands in a greeting. Mr Wilson signaled and one of the policemen walked behind Mohan and kicked him. Mohan fell prostrate at the feet of Mr. Wilson.

A multitude of thoughts flashed through Mohan's mind-he wanted to kill the man then and there but the thought of his young wife all alone with a little kid tied his hands. When he got up he was informed that he was being transferred to work on the tracks in the region of Banda, and refusal to go there was to be treated as a treason.

Mohan invited his brother-in-law to come and live with his family and went to his posting where gang-men were dying like flies either due to cholera or dysentery. A large number of them were being killed by tigers almost on a daily basis. The area surrounding his stretch of tracks passed through a dense forest which was full of wild tuskers, bears, tigers, wolves, poisonous snakes and scorpions, insects with deadly bites, mosquitoes, trees with poisonous fruits, and robbers. Mohan slept in an open tent, with only his lathi to protect him. Somehow this close encounter with death on a daily basis doused his anger. He survived in the forest by sheer luck and respect for the privacy of the wild animals.

About six months later he got a leave. He took a train and reached the station which was about twelve kilometers from his home. He could have waited till morning and taken another train. He looked up at the sky- there were clouds but it was not likely to rain. He decided to walk along the track to reach home.

There was a bridge on the river near his home. When he was still quite some distance away he saw movement on the bridge. Some men were attaching some equipment to the track while two persons stood with pistols at the two ends of the bridge, keeping guard. They were working in dark. Mohan hid behind a bush and waited. Their work done the men left hurriedly on three motor cycles.

The memory of the humiliation caused by Mr. Wilson was his companion, he was still being punished by being posted away from his family, and he was not oblivious to all the injustice which the British rule had wrought in India. Yet he knew that the blowing of the bridge would cast innocent lives. He collected two sticks, tore his red turban into two and stretched one of them across the track. Then he crossed the river and stretched the other half on the other side as well. He could see his home from where he stood. He knew that if the men found that he had seen them they would come after him. He was tired after a day-long journey by train and a walk of almost ten kilometers. Yet he crossed the river again and ran to the station where the Permanent Way Inspector lived. Only when he reached the bungalow, around two in the night, did it occur to him that he may have to face Mr.

Wilson, again.

Still he knocked at the imposing gate. A watch man came and looked at him with suspicion. A dog started barking. The watch man recognized Mohan and called the Inspector. A new Inspector named Mr. Harrison had joined recently and he was fairly mild mannered. Mr. Harrison listened to Mohan in silence, called some policemen asked Mohan to wait at his bungalow where he was given some tea and proceeded to the bridge on a trolley. They diffused the bomb and saw a train pass by safely.

Mr. Harrison tried to get Mohan rewarded. Mohan refused to accept any reward but requested that he be transferred back to his earlier station. It was arranged by the end of the day. Mr Harrison was also a generous man, he promoted Mohan to the level of a watch-man for the bridge.

Mr. Harrison often stopped by the bridge to admire the view of the river, and to look at the crocodiles and the soons (river dolphins) and the forest nearby. He often chatted with Mohan about the weather and the repairs to be done along the bund near the bridge. He valued Mohan's judgments and never had to regret it. This slowly led to a trust and a sort of friendship whose roots ran deeper than the relation between an officer and a worker.

Several months passed and one day Mohan again went to Mr. Harrison's bungalow. He invited Mr. Harrison to come to a place near his village where some people had started living recently. The land had belonged to a friend of Mohan and he was encouraging people to come and settle there so that the neighbouring forest could be cleared and converted into a farming land. Mr. Harrison had developed a liking for the calm dignified behaviour of Mohan and accepted the invitation. He reached that place in the evening and was greatly moved to know that Mohan had asked his friend to name the upcoming village as "Harrison Ganj".

However, this is not the end of our story. The job of a watchman is not fun by any means. Imagine the rainy season and imagine spending night after night, sitting in an open tent near the bridge with the water from the river always splashing against the banks, trying to erode them and succeeding every now and then when a huge chunk of soil would drop in the river with a big splash along with the trees growing upon it. It is quite common to have crocodiles in that river and they do swim along, and occasionally come to rest just a few feet away from you. And imagine rains lashing against your tent along with a strong gust of wind, when the only sound you hear is that of the wind howling through the trees across the river and across the fields and through the forest. And imagine the burning ghat (the cremation ground) just a few feet away from the bridge on the other side with its peepal tree-its leaves rattling in the slightest breeze. It requires courage and faith in oneself to sit alone in such surroundings all alone, year after year without losing one's bearings. Mohan had one confidence, just one faith-he had never harmed any-one knowingly and the only occasion when he had thought of killing someone, namely Mr. Wilson-he had controlled himself. So he sat there in his tent, singing bhajans while it was rained heavily all around him.

A huge splash told him that the river had cut away yet another chunk of soil near the bank and the huge tree had also fallen in the river. He was used to seeing the river rise by several feet during such rains within a night. So he was not surprised when he saw the water in one of the channels leading to the river rise. However, he soon realized that some-thing was amiss, as the sound of the rain and the wind was broken by loud yelps and a hissing sound. He realized that the water must have entered the cave-like alcove on the wall-face near the channel where a family of wolves had taken shelter for the last several weeks. He came out, holding his lantern under his rain-coat to see that only the male wolf had survived and rest of the family of was being carried away by the swiftly flowing river. He saw the wolf standing there on the bank of the river, fidgeting and howling and making heart rendering noises.

He came back to his tent and waited for the rains to stop. He must have dozed off. He woke-up to see the wolf sitting in a corner of the tent. Even though Mohan knew that wolves are carnivores, he threw a chapati at the wolf. The wolf jumped up with a start and started growling. Mohan just sat there. His quiet convinced the wolf that he meant no harm. Towards morning when the rain subsided, the wolf left.

From that day on, when-ever it rained, the wolf came and took shelter in the tent of Mohan. On his part Mohan was happy for a company, any company, and he often talked to the wolf, telling him of his days at the back-breaking work as a gang-man, and his humiliation at the hands of Mr. Wilson, of his days in the forests of Banda, and of the generosity of Mr. Harrison and of his son who was studying to be a doctor. And then a time came when the wolf started coming to sit in his tent even when it was not raining and a bond of trust and friendship grew between Mohan and the wolf. Some-times the wolf vanished for several days but if it was in the neighbourhood it always paid Mohan a visit.

Two years passed, India became free, Mr. Harrison emigrated to New Zealand and it was rainy season again. It was raining heavily, the visibility was quite poor. Mohan put up the signals at the bridge for the trains to pass slowly, very-very slowly, as the river was in full spate. And he stood in the rain, holding his lantern waving to the train.

The Punjab Mail was several hours late and it was almost eleven in the night. Two babus sat near the window, right under the sign which stated, “Consumption of alcohol is prohibited” and were busy with their drinks and guffaws. It was then that they noticed that their bottle was empty, they were angry and looked out. They saw this man standing in the rain, waving his lantern. It was such a delight for them to aim their bottle at his head.

Mohan fell down, the train went by with the babus happy in their glorious victory and Mohan bled. The wolf watched and stood guard over him, snapping at the jackals which had collected. In the morning when Mohan did not return home at his usual time, my mother-his wife-sent me to find out. I brought him home with the help of some friends. I had not noticed but my friends saw a wolf hiding in the bushes near the bridge and their first reaction was that perhaps the wolf had injured him. My father was quite conscious though he had lost a lot of blood. He shouted at them to leave the wolf alone. My mother nursed him to health and he rejoined duty.

And till he stayed home we saw the wolf often near our home, just outside the reach of the dogs late in the evenings. And you may verify it from the passengers of the trains which passed that bridge during the night that for several years the wolf ran after each and every train, growling and growling, and perhaps, as the people say, looking for the jokers who had injured Mohan.

And if you ask the older people around, they would tell you that the bridge which is now called “Neta Manohar Lal Bridge” was once called the 'Wolf Bridge'. But then Harrison Ganj is also called Hari Sen Ganj now and the new breed of traders and babus who have started living there due to the thriving carpet industry in the neighbourhood have completely forgotten its origin in the devotion to duty and the trust and friendship of a simple, dignified and silent Indian and a just Englishman. But then who cares for history any-way.

7

Song of the Lonely Doe

His name was Madhaee. Actually it was Madhava Das but Eastern Uttar Pradesh has a way of softening all the sharp edges of every word and every person. Thus he became Madhaee, his name suitably distorted to enable our teachers to call him in a scornful manner, e.g. Madhaeeya, every now and then to carry out odd jobs. He became my class-mate when I reached the second standard. He was in the second standard for the two previous years.

We studied in the Primary School of Bholaganj on the Grand Trunk Road. The school at Raniganj was more than eight miles away and so we had kids often walking up-to four miles to reach the school. Madhaee's father worked in our fields and nursed a dream to educate him to be a khalaasi (a sort of porter cum peon) with the railways. During some moment of generousity-a trait quite absent in him, my father had offered this dream to him and also offered to help Madhaee with books etc. which normally meant that he would get the old books of my elder brother. He also introduced his father to the station master of the railway station near the school. In those golden days an education up-to fifth standard and a bribe of just five hundred rupees were enough to get you a job as a 'casual' khalaasi with the railways.

Madhaee's father would often go to the station master of the small station near our school with some produce from the fields, like sugar-cane juice, or green peas, or potatoes and sweet potatoes, or pumpkins, or otherwise curd, or ghee, or honey, or else mangoes etc. to keep this hope alive. But Madhaee was proving difficult. He was 'refusing' to learn to read or write.

When I joined him in class two, I was surprised that he could just about recognize the Devnagari alphabets. My brother had passed out from the primary school and thus it was decided that I would travel to school with him. The school was about two miles away and we walked there together. Once I was ready, my grandfather would shout for Madhaee whose house was not very far. He would come running and we would start our walk together.

This was real fun with a variety of adventures to which he introduced me on the way. While going we were always in a hurry to reach in time so our adventures were limited to sightings of snakes and foxes, and collection of blobs of gum from babool trees, and ber, kaitha, tamarind, and mangoes from the trees on the way. We also had to cross a shallow river which was easy enough, as we would strip to our waste, raise the satchel, the takhti (the wooden writing slate) and the stone writing slate, over our head and wade across. If the water level was higher, he would lift me on his shoulders and take me across. On our way back we often 'stole' sugar-cane or green peas and green gram from the fields. On such occasions I would act as a look-out while he collected the 'booty'. We also ate the piquant green leaves of the plants of gram (chane ka saag) with salt and chilli and collected quills of porcupines and feathers of peacocks. Madhaee was very good at spotting the precise spots where a sweet potato could be found in the fields and we stole them, washed them in the river and ate them before being caught! These shared adventures slowly led to a deep bond of affection between us. The most important "job" we did on the way was to collect reeds for making pens and to offer a prayer to Pehelwan Veer Baba to save us from the punishments of the teacher.

None of the teachers of our school had a watch and our school would formally start when the passenger train going from Benares to Lucknow reached the railway station. Some-times when it looked that it was time for the school to start even though the train had not come, our Head Master would make a guess by looking at the shadow cast by the school building. The school started with an assembly and a prayer. The prayer was always led by Madhaee as he had the sweetest and the most melodious voice and the clearest pronunciation of the Sanskrit verses used in the prayer.

Our first job was to prepare our takhtis for sulekh or hand-writing. This was an art. We would go to the neighbouring pond with some soot from oil lamps or black powder from used dry battery cells and apply it on the wooden slates with some water. Then we would start swinging them to make them dry, singing, " O! my sandal-wood takhti, get dry quickly, The teacher is waiting, cane in hand..."

Once the slates were dry we would rub the black coating off the takhtis with the smooth edge of a small bottle, till it shined. And then using a thread and a piece of khadia mitti (chalk) we would draw rulings on them. This was also an art. We wrapped the thread between the left fore-finger and the toe of the right leg. And then we rubbed the chalk on the thread, holding it taut. Next, squatting on the ground, we placed the takhti on our left thigh and leg, stretching the thread over it rather closely and then striking the thread somewhat like striking a string on an ek-tara-a single stringed musical instrument popular with fakirs. It left a white straight line on the takhti. Several parallel lines were thus created on it and then we dissolved chalk in little pots and used the pens made from reed which we had picked while coming to school to copy out some passage from our book.

We waited till the writing was dry and then we stood in a queue in front of our teacher, saying prayers to Pehelwan Veer Baba and hoping that the teacher would not notice the mistakes and the bad hand-writing. The punishment was severe, one hit with his cane for one mistake, two for two, four for three, and eight for four mistakes! Some-times the teacher would get excited, forget the count, and frothing at his mouth, he would even forget the custom of hitting only on the out-stretched palm and his cane would rain all over the students' bodies. Madhaee was easily the most punished boy in the class. We would wince as Madhaee took hit-upon-hit on his out-stretched palms along with the curses depicting close encounters between the teacher and Madhaee's female relatives-some of them not even born.

I was always amazed at the amount of punishment he could take without crying out in pain and I remember several occasions when the stick used by the teacher broke and Madhaee was asked to bring a fresh stick and the punishments continued. I also used to be amazed that Madhaee never mentioned a desire, even slightest desire, to skip the school for the fear of the punishments.

Let us come back to our studies. After the writing part was over, the monitor of the class would ask us to scatter in the field of the school and shout out the sums. We would write the sums on our stone slates with batti (sand-stone pencils), and take it to him to check it and line-up again for the punishments.

By this time we would have a lunch break. We would rush to the small market near the school where there was a well and a temple. We would go on the roof of the temple and take out our packets of chapatis coated with ghee to be eaten with pickles or vegetables. Some students would bring gram, or rice, or jwar or bajra, and they would take it to the bhujwa who had a huge wok full of sand on a fire of dry leaves. And he would take one third of the grain as payments for puffing it in the hot sand. It was a sheer excitement to see a small amount of rice or bajra ballooning to a large volume of white, fragrant, warm mass of puffed grain.

The students ate the puffed grain with gur or just chilli and salt and drew water from the well to quench their thirst. I would often exchange my ghee coated chapatis for some puffed rice or gram. On such occasions I had to take Madhaee into confidence so that the news of this barter did not reach my mother.

Then we returned to the school and played kabaddi or a game of ball, made of a small bundle of rags. Sometimes we had 'fights' using our terracotta ink-pots where we held our pots in our palms and hit the similarly held pots by our friends. We would also put our takhti inclined against the tree under which the class was held and rolled our reed pens down them. The pens would roll away and when a reed pen rolled by the opponent touched them he won them. Madhaee owned a “champion” reed pen using which he would often win the pens of the entire class, only to return them.

The afternoons were spent in memorizing the

multiplication tables by rote and reading our text book loudly while the class teacher either dozed or gossiped with his colleagues. There was not much of a traffic on the Grand Trunk Road then, but every passing ekka (one horse carriage), or bullock-cart, or camel, or the very rare trucks and the two buses which plied there were objects of our closest possible scrutiny. These disturbances were also followed by random punishments from our teacher.

Now I must tell you the story of his elevation to the level of my protector. Even though my family belonged to one of the upper castes we were not exactly rich. The class was full of sons of rich Brahmins, Thakurs and Kayasthas. I was the youngest kid in the class and also the weakest. This ensured that I was subjected to a lot of bullying during breaks and during my journey to and from the school.

However in the mornings and evenings I had to sit with my mother, while she cooked and had to revise the multiplication tables and read the books to her. In the evenings I had to prepare a takhtiful of writing for my father to see. As a result of these forced studies, soon, I started doing all my sums correctly and was no longer getting any punishments. I started believing that Madhaee was indeed dumb, as our teacher suggested on a daily basis, while I was a brilliant student!

It never occurred to me at that time that while I sat studying with my mother, Madhaee had to clean the shed for our cattle, get them water and fodder, and do all kinds of odd jobs for my grand-father. Even at the school all the teachers were often asking Madhaee to do odd jobs. Even a slightest hesitation on his part used to invite a ridicule from them that a fellow like him, belonging to such a backward caste was aspiring to be a Deputy Collector! I suppose, that was the highest white-collar official our teachers knew.

On the other hand the slow but perceptible change in my 'fortunes' was duly noted by the other students in the class who started threatening me in various ways. Sometimes I used to get so scared that I deliberately made mistakes and took punishments. But one day I was not careful enough and the entire class got punished for not remembering the multiplication table of nineteen, except me. While returning from school one of them picked up a fight with me, cursing my lineage and in the manner of the teacher-my female relatives. I was cornered. Even at that young age-I was perhaps six or seven then-I knew that Madhaee would not be much of a help as he was poor and he came from a backward caste. However, when one of the boys tried to push me down a steep slope into a ravine, he intervened. A fight ensued and once Madhaee got over his reluctance of hitting the upper caste boys in my defense, the fight was over quickly. Normally he would have been severely punished for raising his hands at them but as he did it in 'my defense', it was over-looked by the elders. The bullying stopped.

A few days later I was made the class monitor. I had also realized that Madhaee was not getting enough time to study, so I started teaching him all that I knew on the way to the school, starting with multiplication tables. His performance improved and to the surprise of all he started escaping punishments.

Three years passed. We came to the fifth standard. Madhaee was almost sixteen and had developed a moustache. According to the customs of his community he was already married when he was about two years old. His wife had 'arrived' during the previous summer.

I still remember the day when he invited me to his house to introduce me to his wife. Once the elders left, she removed the veil and a pretty girl with laughter in her eyes faced me. 'So you are the Guru of my husband!', she said and laughed. I did not find anything funny about this but found myself laughing too. That laughter is still etched in my memory.

She often came to our house along with her mother-in-law to help my mother and adopted me as her devar (brother-in-law)-teasing me whenever she found an occasion, any occasion, and threatening to do severe damage to my looks during the festival of Holi, which she did. It took me several days to remove the colours she had poured on me.

She sang well, knew all the songs for all the festive occasions and was always invited all over the village for all kinds of functions. Her real specialty was what we call 'Mangal Geet' which are actually 'gaali' (abuses threaded into lyrical songs)! Lest you feel concerned, in Eastern U. P., during marriages the women from the bride's village sing gaali targeting the relatives of the bridegroom. This is considered to bring good-luck and is thoroughly enjoyed by all and the father of the bride-groom is expected to reward these singers.

Around this time, Madhaee learnt to play flute and to sing folk-songs. His voice had matured a great deal by then. The Head-Master of our school took him under his wings to sing at all school functions. He won the district level award for folk-songs for the school and several awards in athletics.

The final examinations were approaching and we realized that between his wife, his singing, and working with our cattle he had once again neglected his studies. I was called by the Head Master and told that during the examination Madhaee would sit directly behind me, and that I was to hold my answer-books in such a manner that he could copy! I hesitated only slightly before agreeing. Madhaee passed the fifth standard.

His father sold his only cow, his wife sold all her silver ornaments and borrowed some money from my mother. His father went to the station master with the five hundred ruppees. Madhaee was appointed as a 'casual' khalaasi.

I met him every day at the station, where he had started working and from where I took the passenger train to go to the school in the city. I still remember, that he some-times came and sat by my side, touched my books longingly and lovingly, saying nothing.

His wife was spending a lot of time at our house, helping my mother, and she continued to tease me about either not paying any attention to her, or about paying too much attention to her and not to my books. Her laughter filled our house, like the sound of silver bells. My mother found a daughter in her, she never had.

Life was becoming good for Madhaee, who had in the mean-time joined the group of folk dancers of his community who danced and sang on several occasions and were often invited to far-off places. He had a steady income of forty-five ruppees a month from the railways, excluding the compulsory lay-offs once in a while. He worked both at the station and at the quarters of the station master. When there was no work in sight he took out his flute, played on it, and sang wonderful melodious songs. Passers-by stopped, sat down, listened, praised him, and bought a paan for him before going on their way. Madhaee was contended. I was already preparing to move to the hostel at Allahabad University for my further studies which was sure to take me away for long periods of time from home. I suppose, this story should have ended here with each one of us living our own destiny. Well...

It was summer, just after the harvest. A marriage

party came to our village from the city of Allahabad.

One of the important members of the party was the MLA from Allahabad and every-body hovered around him. Madhaee had been called to help with the wedding feast and his wife to sing gaali. A pair of dancing girls from Allahabd had also come with the marriage party. During the night, the dancing girls sang some gaali and soon it turned into a competition between the women of the village and the dancing girls. Every-body stopped eating, once Madhaee's wife started the replies, in her very clear, very sweet and a most melodious voice.

Yes, I remember that night. It was a full moon night. The arrangements for the wedding were done in a field which had been cleared for the occasion. The village women sat with the dhols (drums) behind a 'curtain' of string cots standing on their sides, singing joyously, led by Madhaee's wife. A gathering of almost three hundred people sat spell-bound listening to an illiterate untutored village girl. The cultured and well-dressed dancing girls who had come with the party, and who sang to the accompaniment of tabla, saarangi, and harmonium were all but forgotten.

The MLA showed a lot of appreciation and called Madhaee's wife to reward her. He also said that he was like a father to her and that she should remove the veil. Egged-on by the people trying to please him, she obliged. I was not sure that I saw a fatherly expression on his face and felt very uneasy. However, there were too many things going on and I got busy with the wedding.

But that was the last time that we saw her alive. In the morning, we found her dead in a corner of the house where the wedding had taken place, apparently of a snake-bite. There was a big uproar but it subsided when a 'doctor' who had come with the wedding party 'confirmed' that she had really died of 'snake-bite'.

Madhaee was a completely changed person after this. He stopped singing, took to smoking ganja (marijuana) and no one ever saw a smile on his face. One day while he sat with me at the railway station, sitting silently and yet conveying a lot, I saw a black thread around his neck. It looked like a taabeej (talisman) tied in a small piece of red cloth. 'It is only a token of your sister-in-law's memory', he said, when he found me looking at it and then buttoning up his shirt up-to the neck, he just stared blankly at some far-away point near the horizon.

One year passed. I came home again during the summer vacations. It must have been beyond mid-night. We were awakened by a very sad song coming from Madhaee's house, followed by the saddest melody played on the flute. Who can easily forget that cry of pain; 'the song of the lonely doe' well-known in our part of the country-side:

“The hunter has killed the deer and made a dhapali (a hand-held flat drum) from its skin”, the song goes,

“And now,
When anyone plays the dhapali,.
The doe gets restless...
Have you not seen her?
Standing by the watering-hole,
Flooding it with her tears,..”

My mother wept, recalling that it was the first anniversary of the death of Madhaee's wife. She also said that as far as she knew this was the first time after her death that Madhaee was singing.

In the morning some-one brought a news that the

MLA from Allahabad had been murdered in the Allahabad-Lucknow passenger train which passed close to our village around mid-night. Within an hour of this news reaching us, police came, led by a pair of sniffer dogs. They headed straight for Madhaee's house. According to the custom of the police of Eastern Uttar Pradesh, they started beating him mercilessly even before they asked him a question, while the dogs barked at him. In the melee the taabeej around his neck broke. The police-inspector picked it up and untied the knot. Many of us recognized the large gold ring which the MLA had worn during the wedding, his name engraved on it.

I met Madhaee on the day before he was hanged. "Your sister-in-law was here last night", he said.

And then he added, "She asked me to tell you that she died with her honour intact. She also said that she will be there to sing gaali during your wedding!"

And he smiled, a smile of relief from an excruciating pain.

8

Droit du Seigneur

I had not met my sister's family for three years. I took the evening train to her village, which got severely delayed. I had no idea how late it was as I had left my watch at home knowing that I was to travel during night. A near full moon was up and a cool breeze was blowing. I decided to walk the three miles-the alternative was to sleep on the stone bench on the deserted railway platform till morning. The narrow dirt road from the station went straight to her village, my brother-in-law had often taken me there on his motor-bike.

The plants of wheat had grown to a height of almost a feet and looked beautiful, swaying in the gentle breeze, dazzling in the moon-light. But for an occasional fox and a solitary jackal I did not meet any one for the first mile or so. Then I saw a large building, newly painted, looking like a school in the middle of a vast near barren field, which I recalled was called 'The Salt Fields'. I remembered seeing a small mud house at its place during my earlier visit. I assumed that the school must have come up during the intervening period. I was happy, as my sister's village did not have a proper school and her children stayed with our parents at Allahabad for their studies.

Reaching closer I saw an old man in khadi kurta, dhoti, and Gandhi cap, sitting on a little mound, looking at the building and smoking hukkah. He had made a little fire of dry leaves and some wood to keep himself warm. I assumed that he was the watch-man. I wished him and asked him if he was. His reply aroused my curiousity. Instead of saying 'yes or no', he said, 'you could call me that'.

I joined him for a little rest and some warmth from the fire and told him where I was going. He knew my brother-in-law's family and gave me their news. We chatted and when I told him that I lived in Calcutta he told me of his stay there in late-forties and early fifties. He had wonderful memories of the city. Then he expressed a mild surprise that I had not recognized him, as he was Munshi Kanhaiya Lal. And I remembered.

* * *

Munshiji originally came from a relatively well to do family. When the first three children born of his parents died in childhood he was 'sold' for a token amount of one ruppee to his aunt right after birth and she took him away and raised him. This act was believed to confuse the goddess of fate. However, whether because of this or because of the better medical facilities in the city of Lucknow, where his aunt lived, Munshiji survived and grew up to get a good education. He was the first person from the village to study up to high school. When his father took him to meet the Raja of the princely state to which his village belonged, he was offered a job as a teacher for the children of high officials of the palace. He was to be an assistant to the Anglo-Indian teachers who prepared the children for admission to school especially created for them in the hills of Himalayas. His job came with the title of Munshiji, which he was to retain for the rest of his life.

The Raja, even though old and lame, was quite a debaucher. His life was one long party, with dancing girls called from Lucknow and Benares, wine and scotch brought from Calcutta, where in turn it was brought from Europe, and opium imported from Afghanistan.

Munshiji had grown-up in the city of Lucknow which was under the influence of Arya Samaj as well as the movements of the Congress against the British rule. He had also 'flirted a bit' with the revolutionaries, but somehow the news had reached his mother and aunt, and all his inclinations in that direction were drowned in their tears. Yet, the revolt against the oppression stayed just under the surface.

The palace officials were invariably quite haughty and it was common for them to beat up the tenant-farmers on some excuse or to race their horses in their fields on some pretext just to keep them frightened. Munshiji was a marked man when he objected to this practice on several occasions. Knowing that the Raja used to see Munshiji once in a while to help him draft some petitions to the King of England, the palace officials waited and bided their time.

It was well known that his wife was very pretty. He received hints from the cronies of the Raja to bring her to one of the numerous parties which he gave. Munshiji knew well what went on there and avoided. Then one day he was told explicitly to bring her to the party being organized to celebrate the advent of spring, Basant

Panchami. He stayed home. The news of his 'disobedience' was conveyed to the Raja. The palace guards went to fetch both of them. Perhaps they were drunk, or perhaps they were told to punish them, or perhaps they wanted to make an example of them. They pulled them out of their house. Munshiji offered some resistance while his wife jumped in the well and killed herself. People assembled. They were told that Munshiji had stolen jewels from the palace! No one believed the guards. However, the villagers were too scared to protest.

Anyone else would have easily lost his life, but Munshiji, was fairly well known. And there was the English Resident always on a look-out for the 'misdeeds' of the Raja. It was also rumoured that any such 'finding' always made him richer.

However Munshiji was accused of colluding with the freedom fighters, an act which the English Resident was bound to punish severely. Once accused, Munshiji found a drastic change in the attitude of the white police-inspector. He suffered terribly at the hands of the police-men who tried to extract the names of his 'collaborators'. When a month of regular beatings at irregular intervals and a denial of sleep did not yield any information, the police-inspector realized that Munshiji was falsely implicated.

He relaxed the guard on him. After waiting for fifteen more days, Munshiji escaped through the hatch of the latrine through which the sweeper used to carry the night-soil away. He crawled through the excrements of his fellow prisoners. It was still dark and he hid in a pond near the railway station, staying in the thick growth of water-plants. He waited for the washer-men to appear while leeches feasted upon him. He stole a saree from the clothes spread-out to dry in the sun, pulled a long veil, went to a bangle shop and fled after stealing some bangles.

Later in the evening he got into a train going to Calcutta and hid in the toilet. During this time the news of his escape had spread. The police and the palace guards were furious. They went to his village and the first thing they did was to severely assault his parents. When they could not provide any hints about the where-abouts of Munshiji, the palace guards burned down his house, and in an act of ultimate insult, ploughed the land where his house had stood using a plough pulled by two asses. Next, they got several bullock-cart loads of salt and spread it over his fields. Nothing was to grow there for several decades, and his land was to become known as 'The Salt Fields' for all time to come.

Hiding in the toilet of the train, Munshiji heard the passengers talk of this in hushed tones and was dazed at the speed at which the events had taken place. Somehow he came out of the train at Howrah and stole cloths again. Then he worked, first as a coolie and then as an accountant. When he heard of a ship going to Rangoon he took that and worked his way to Rangoon. He lived there under an assumed name till the freedom of India was clearly in sight. He participated extensively in organizing support for the freedom struggle, and later for the Indian National Army.

He met Netaji Subhash Chandra Bose at a meeting. Several years earlier, I had seen a faded framed photograph in his house with Netaji surrounded by a crowd. One of the heads had belonged to Munshiji. During the same visit he had also given me several bills amounting to a few thousand ruppees, issued by the Japanese army when it had occupied Burma and had shown me his secret seal with his actual name in elegant Gothic Script around a symbol which he had told was his name in Japanese.

Netaji was very happy with him and during a meeting had suggested that upon return to India he should open a school for the children. That was the first time when Munshiji was treated with respect and with courtesy by some-one so important. A memory of those few moments gave him enormous courage in years to come.

He returned to Calcutta a little before Netaji vanished. He was waiting for the things to settle down to return to his village. He had come to know that the old Raja had died, without any children. A distant relative's son had been adopted to succeed him and the new Raja's father who had appointed himself as advisor to him, had replaced almost all the employees by his trusted men. His one hope was that in free India the minions of the new Raja may not bother him. He was not wrong as they had busied themselves in stripping the palace of wealth accumulated over centuries.

India became free. By some miracle he escaped the Great Calcutta Killings, and offered one gold sovereign to the deity at the Kalighat Temple when Mahatma Gandhi gave up his fast. Thirty-six years after his arrest he returned to his village.

He found that his fields were still barren. He came to know that the manner of the death of his wife had scared people and no-one had tried to usurp it. There was also a talk that the spirits of his wife and unborn son haunted the area where his house and the fields had been. His parents had died soon after that incident.

He contacted his cousins at Lucknow, built a small house and started living where his large house had once stood. Years of living alone with only memories, had made him rather self-sufficient. He was well beyond his middle age then. However, as he had accumulated wealth he received several proposals from poor parents of young girls. He firmly said no. After some initial persuasion his close relatives were secretly happy about it as they expected to inherit the lands. To the surprise of all, the sighting of the spirits stopped even though Munshiji did keep awake, night after night, for just a glimpse of his wife who had served as a guardian of his lands for so many years.

Finding his funds running out, Munshiji carefully flooded and then drained his fields and loaded it with cow-dung purchased from the villagers. In the beginning nothing much happened but slowly some grain started growing. Soon, several people started asking him to take his land on adhia (half), a scheme under which where they were to work on his land and give half of the produce to him.

Munshiji was free again. He decided to keep his promise to Netaji Subhas Bose and expressed his intention to open a school. In the beginning people laughed and none of the kids who went to a school, about four miles away came to him. He decided to give them free coaching, in the evenings. This some-how worked as the performance of his students improved. However they were the children of rich farmers. The children of landless labourers roamed around doing nothing, or grazing cattle, or cutting grass, or helping their parents who worked in the fields of the rich farmers. Munshiji decided to educate them. This led to serious problems, problems he had never envisaged.

When the rich farmers found their cheap labour missing and sitting in the verandah of Munshiji, they called a meeting of the village council. Serious debate ensued. You can easily imagine, who said what. The verdict was simple, while Munshiji was welcome to tutor the children of the rich farmers, he was expected to keep away from the children of landless labourers. 'If they also got educated-who would work in the fields'-was the simple refrain.

When Munshiji refused to obey the dictate, his class-room was destroyed and the books he had brought for the kids were burnt. He had not realized that one Raja was now replaced by several rich farmers, who were out to have their way by all means, fair or foul. He was asked to obey the dictate else he was to be ex-communicated, the heaviest penalty the council could impose.

Even though he had worked actively for Netaji, he had never lost his reverence for Mahatma Gandhi. He refused to obey the dictate. He added that he had promised to Netaji that he would run a school in his village, and so he would! He was ex-communicated. No one was to talk to him. He was not to be given water by any-one, the barber was not to cut his hair, the washer-man was not to wash his clothes and no-one was to work in his field. He was not to go near the well.

Yes, that story was well-known. They had not reckoned with the obstinacy of Munshiji. He went to the city and paying an enormous sum, got some people to bore a hand-pump near his house, denying him-self water till it worked at the end of the day. He also brought a new black-board, a pictorial chart of numerals and alphabets and a world map! He set up the class-room again. He washed his own clothes, cut his own hair, cooked his own meals, washed his utensils, and sat on a chair-day-after-day waiting for his students to return. None came.

A month passed, and he still set up the class every day and waited. Even the upper class boys did not come to him for coaching. And then he decided to have a school for adults. He went around the village and talked to the untouchables and most backward castes and encouraged them to come to him to read. They laughed but came. He read from Ramayan for them and wrote letters for them and listened to their problems and succeeded in convincing them that they could indeed learn to read and write.

A single-minded determination has its own way of affecting people. The kids started coming to him again, he spotted the bright ones and the school started again but on the compromise that it was to run only in the evenings so that the children of the land-less labourers remained available for working in the fields. He knew that he could not improve their lot, but they could read and write and keep accounts and they could even read what the village-trader wrote in his bahi khaataa (the account-book) against their name.

Then in sixties the government decided to open a primary school in his village. The villagers were quite surprised to know that the land which was supposed to be panchayat's land, had some-how been transferred to the village-chief. No land was found where a school could be held. Munshiji came forward, and offered half of his lands to the government to open the school. He even offered some funds to build the school by selling a large part of the remaining land.

I looked at Munshiji, he was looking wistfully at the white painted school building while a glow of satisfaction played on his face. 'Yes, it is good school', he said. 'It has very good and sincere teachers and every one comes to the school', he added.

I had sat for long with him. I wished him and asked for leave.

By the time I reached my sister's house the Venus was up on the eastern sky. They were pleasantly surprised and my sister went to prepare some tea. My youngest nephew, who was still at home had woken up and talked incessantly about the gifts I had taken for him. While taking tea I told my brother-in-law of my meeting with Munshiji on the way. He smiled and asked me to rest.

By the time I was up again, the sun was shining. My brother-in-law was ready with his tractor to carry sugar-cane to the sugar-mill which had opened nearby. He invited me to go with him.

The track followed the route I had taken the previous night, till we reached the Salt Fields. I saw the mound where I had talked to Munshiji. Right in front, stood a building, half collapsed, where I had seen a large school building during the night. 'This is Munshiji's School', my brother-in law whispered softly.

Noticing my shock he told that once Munshiji offered his land for the building for the school, posts for several teachers were sanctioned. The village chief had four daughters-in-law who had some education. Some 'certificates' were arranged and they were appointed as teachers at the school. By then the government sanctioned money to erect a building for the school. Munshiji was very excited and he talked to the Public Works Department men who came to build the school in detail about the lay-out etc. He even offered some money towards this. The building was made, the students and the villagers were asked to help and they did. It was just a coincidence that a very nice brick and cement out-house was built in front of the house of the village chief at the same time. We had seen it on our way.

My brother-in-law continued. Two years earlier, on the Independence Day, the school building was inaugurated. In the evening Munshiji went to market to bask in the glory of a dream full-filled. Yes, he was very happy that day. On the way back it had started raining heavily. He took shelter in the school.

His body was found, buried under the debris of the collapsed school building in the morning.

* * *

The full realization of the sufferings and struggles of Munshiji had hit me like a railway engine and I was stunned. We remained silent for a long time after my brother-in-law finished.

It took me quite some time to recover. I recalled how horrified I had felt when I had asked 'Munshiji' during the night as to why he had not tried to start a family again.

He had looked at the yellowing moon and had kept quiet for long. And then he had told me in a barely audible whisper that when he was first arrested by the palace guards, he had been castrated before being handed over to the white police.

9

Lotus in the Land of Edelweiss

I first met Walter at the Benares Hindu University. I had gone to attend an international conference there, which he was also attending. We had started chatting while helping ourselves with the food when I made a suggestion to him to keep away from the salads. The organizers had arranged a boat-ride next day. It was a large double-decker boat, where the boat-men pulled the oars on the lower deck and we sat on chairs on the deck above.

It was a pleasant February morning when we started at Assi Ghat and I was soon joined by Walter. We sat there watching people take a bath, listening to bells of temples, feeding the water-birds which followed our boat, and looking at the vast flowering mustard fields on the other side of the river. It was then that Walter asked me about the ghats. I told him of the history of the ghats-Tulsi Ghat where Goswami Tulsi Das had lived and written the epic Ram Charit Manas, the Chet Singh Ghat from where

Maharaja Chet Singh had jumped into the swollen Ganges, when pursued by British soldiers to escape to Ramnagar. I pointed out the Jantar Mantar where the Maharaja of Jaipur had built his observatory. I told him of Shankaracharya and Kabir and of how Ahilyabai rebuilt the Vishwanath Temple and Maharaja Ranjitsingh covered it with gold. And I told him of the story associated with the Harischandra Ghat. We talked about the first preaching of Buddha at Sarnath.

Seeing him looking at a drain emptying into the Ganges I told him the story of Lompada (the man with a hairy sole!), who was a contemporary of Buddha, and who had never come down from his bed, leading to a growth of hair on his soles. It was said that when he took a bath, the drains of Kashi used to overflow with saffron. Both of us laughed at the change in the nature of effluent over the centuries while the human nature remained unchanged. And we talked of Madan Mohan Malaviya who had single-handedly built the university and explained the most sacred mantras to untouchables, in his personal fight against untouchability. He listened with attention and then commented, "Sunanda will miss this".

I asked him about Sunanda. It turned out that a few years earlier he and his wife had seen a programme on television about the work being done by an orphanage in Calcutta and had decided to adopt a child from there. Their own children were much older and had moved to hostels. After several trips to India they were allowed to take Sunanda with them to Germany.

About four years later I went to Germany with my family. We had kept in touch-exchanging cards and occasional letters. Walter invited us to visit him. He was at the station with Sunanda. Our daughter was a bit older and my son a bit younger to Sunanda. They had picked up sufficient German by then. The three children immediately started chattering away to our delight. Walter had a huge house with several bed-rooms at the foot-hills of a little mountain near the edge of a forest. The nearest neighbour lived almost half a kilometer away. Walter had made a garden house for Sunanda where she took our children and they appeared only when we shouted for them to have lunch. And they vanished again to make castles and cars from lego and to paint.

My children had never gone to bed before listening to a story. My son always sat on my belly, while my daughter hugged me while I told the stories. Some-where along the story my son would lie on my chest and fall asleep.A little later our daughter would also fall asleep. That evening we faced a problem. My knowledge of German has remained quite poor. Sunanda spoke only German. So my children offered to do a running translation. Now my son sat on my belly, my daughter hugged me from one side and Sunanda hugged me from the other side. And thus we started our story session. I used to tell stories either from Ramayan, or Mahabharat, or Panchatantra, or some fairly tale. That day I told them the story of a jackal who had fallen in a tub of coloured water, which had rendered his tail blue, and his subsequent adventures. Walter followed the laughter to the guest room and saw us. He sat listening while the children slowly fell asleep. Then he took Sunanda away to her separate bed-room. Before leaving he said, "Sunanda will miss this."

During the night I and my wife talked about Sunanda who was definitely lucky to be with Walter, while thousands of children in Calcutta foraged through garbage dumps looking for pieces of bread and rotting vegetables and plastic bags and paper. Yet, strange that it may sound, we were feeling bad that Sunanda would grow up without knowing much about India or any of the Indian languages. It was quite late when a mixture of sadness and gratitude exhausted us and we fell asleep.

Next morning the kids raced and competed with each other in finishing the milk given to them and swam with Walter in their in-house swimming pool. After lunch we went out for a walk in the city gardens. While I, my wife, and Walter walked slowly on an oak-lined walk-way, the children raced, giggling and laughing. I remember that day. I was wearing an over-coat and my son would often run back and hide into it, yelling 'cuckoo'. On such occasions it was difficult for me to walk and Walter looked at me with some anxiety. However, soon my daughter and Sunanda also started taking turns at hiding either with me or with my wife. It was then that Walter remarked to my wife, "To any-one looking it must be quite clear that you have three children!" We were both startled at the remark and strangely when we looked at fifty or sixty kids playing there, Sunanda looked closest to us.

A day later we returned. Walter and Sunanda were at the station again. I reached out and held Sunanda in a close hug. I felt a lump rising in my throat as the train moved. Walter again said, "Sunanda will miss you all". She had apparently asked them during the night that why she looked like us and not like them, while our children did look like us. How could I tell her that from the time of Lord Krishna, adopted children have asked this question from their fosterparents.

Several years later I passed through Germany again. I called Walter and enquired about his wife and Sunanda. "Yes, Sunanda is doing well", he said, "Only she is very poor in mathematics. My wife thinks that this is so because she is an Indian."

I wanted to talk with Sunanda. She was not home. She did not remember our visit several years earlier, I was told. I wish I could just tell her, “Sunanda, you may not speak any Indian language and even if we meet we may not be able to talk. You have never been to India after you were brought to Germany and yet you will always be treated as an Indian. The mother who put you in a cradle out-side the orphanage uprooted you from a soil which you may never find again. I do not know what her compulsions were. Yet, I wish to tell you that we will always have a corner in our heart for a child who laughed with our children and who looked so-much like them one day. Sunanda, my daughter is also poor in mathematics but we tell her that she does not work hard enough. Sunanda, you could do with-out this comment.”

“Hello, are you there?”, Walter asked me from the other end. And I hung up.

10

The Scar

Holi was over. Several people from our village had started planning to go either to Ayodhya or to one of the Shitala temples, during the Navaratri. Small pox is now eradicated in our country. But not long ago, Shitala, the goddess of small pox, descended upon our village, every year, and laid some to rest. The lucky ones like me, were branded for life. You can see the mark left by Her in the middle of my forehead, right at the spot where my mother applied the sandal wood paste during festivals.

Yes, I had heard the story several times. No one had expected me to live. The Vaidyajee had come, seen me, and had left-without saying a word. My mother had started crying. And my uncle had climbed the neem tree to pluck fresh leaves, with which he fanned me, while my mother boiled some to wash my wounds. And then my grandmother had taken a bath, carried a pitcher- full of fresh water to the neem tree, considered to be the abode of the goddess and addressed the goddess, requesting her to leave me. In return she was to take me for a visit to Her temple, offer Her a saree and feed several people. And then she had waited. I had recovered consciousness a little later and slowly the wounds had healed, including the ones on my eyes, which were threatening to blind me. I was two, then.

Years passed. And every year after Holi, my grandmother reminded us of her promise to the goddess. My father had found some excuse or other to postpone the visit by one more year-every year, till it was time for me to leave for Allahabad for higher studies. A threat by my grandmother to go on a hunger strike if I was not sent with her to the temple before leaving, solved the issue and my father, who had scant regard for such 'superstitions', yielded.

We took an evening train to the little town where the temple stood a few kilometres down the Ganges at the edge of a forest. It was late when our train reached there and we joined the large number of people spending the night outside the railway station. We spread a bed sheet on the ground, settled in semi-darkness, and rested. I got some water and my grandmother meaded some sattu which we ate with pickles and green chillies. My lip-smacking drew the attention of an old lady who sat near-by and who was accompanied by a young girl, who was twelve or fourteen years old. To say the least she was pretty and playful. She called me 'Bhaiya' and called my grandmother 'Aajii', in the tradition of north Indian villages. She soon joined us on our bed sheet and gave a little head massage to my grandmother, chirping all along and was blessed profusely by her.

Noting her sweet voice, we asked her if she could sing. The old lady cajoled her and soon we were treated to delightful songs, describing the glory of Mother Ganges, Lord Shiva, and longing of a young bride whose husband was away to Calcutta to make money.

We got up early and walked to the Ganges. The old lady and the young girl, Sugni (a baby parrot), tagged on to us. After some haggling we took a boat and started drifting down -stream. It was a wonderful morning. For some time we heard only the sound of the oars, till some-one started a song. This was perhaps enough of a hint for Sugni, who burst into songs. I still remember some of them, describing the longing for a beloved; “O! Mother Ganges, I will offer you a yellow silk saree, send my beloved to me”, a prayer for the recovery of a child; “O! Mother Shitala, blind my child and he will beg at your temple, but let him live, ” and a longing for a child; “O! Lord Shiva, even a swine looks graceful when little piglets run around her, grant me a child. ”

I lay down at the edge of the boat and looked at her, singing joyously. She looked so graceful in her saree for girls, her hair glowing against the rising sun. I put my hand into the water, and let my fingers run through it. A large school of fish followed our boat and birds flew overhead. Golden stalks of ripening wheat and barley could be seen as for as the eyes could reach, when we reached a bend in the river.

There, on a high mound we saw a huge ruin which must have been a haveli, someday. The old lady accompanying Sugni told us the story of that haveli. No one remembered how long it had stood there, but everyone had heard about it. And it was almost a tradition to narrate the story, when one passed by.

“It had belonged to a very rich merchant. Once his son was affected by small pox (she used the word Mata (Mother), for small pox, through-out the narrative). When his condition deteriorated, the merchant stood in the Ganges and made a promise to Shitala that he would pay her a visit and build a temple for her. His son survived and he forgot all about it. The goddess came to him as an Old Brahmin and reminded him of his promise. He laughed and did not comply. Then Mother Ganges approached him in the form of an Old Sanyasi and reminded him of his promise. He laughed as he knew that small pox rarely strikes a person twice. The Sanyasi reminded him that he had made the promise, standing in the Ganges. He laughed again, saying that his stone haveli stood on a high mound and Ganges could not reach there. The Sanyasi smiled and advised him to protect his wealth against thieves and left– rather vanished."

The story continued. We only heard the sound of the oars, the laboured breathing of the boatmen, and cries of water birds. "The merchant took all his gold coins and put them in hollowed beams of wood and covered the ceiling of the highest room of his haveli with them. Rains came. Water in the Ganges rose and it kept rising till it reached the ware-house in the basement. Soon his wares were being sucked into the Ganges.

Then the water entered his cow-shed and all the cows floated down the River. There was sound of crashing all around, and it was not before he saw his wife, son, and the servants being carried by the River. The water entered the highest room, the roof fell and all the wooden beams, stuffed with gold coins, floated down the Ganges. He remembered the visits of the Sanyashi and the Brahmin, asked for forgiveness, and somehow held on to a projection on the wall. He survived, the water receded a day later, and he saw his haveli, devoid of all his wealth, and all his people. He sold his diamond ring and other ornaments which he was wearing and gave the money to the village priest to erect a temple for goddess Shitala and left for Kashi, walking along the Ganges, begging on the way, and living like a sanyasi. He reached Kashi, about twenty days later.

Walking in the market and begging for food, he stood in front of a sweet shop. Someone had given him an adhanna (half of an anna), which he offered to the shop-owner for puffed chick-peas. It was then that he noticed the wooden beams, kept in the sun to dry. People of Kashi have collected wood from the swollen Ganges for centuries to use them as fire wood. He counted the beams, they were all there. He requested the shop-owner to get one of them and unfastened the hidden lever, – outpoured the gold-coins. The shop-owner fell at the feet of the 'sanyasi' and offered it back to him. The merchant told that if Mother Ganges had wanted him to keep them, she would not have taken them away along with his family, and walked away-munching the chick-peas, to live out the punishment given to him by Ganges and Shitala."

All had fallen silent, we could see the haveli, now behind us, and wondered how it must have felt, losing all in an evening, to the same Ganges, which was flowing so gently, so beautifully. Suddenly Sugni screamed and almost jumped over me, in the process rolling me over. We heard a snapping sound and noticed a crocodile, close to the boat. It had just missed my hand which was till recently hanging by the side of the boat, fondling the waters of the Ganges. Her glass bangles broke, several pieces pierced my right arm and it started bleeding. My grandmother took some lime from one of the passengers and tied it on the wound with a piece of cloth. The bleeding stopped.

Slowly the excitement died down. We had left the crocodile far behind. Every one praised the bravery of Sugni. It was then that I noticed that she did not have any sign of encounter with small pox. I was curious and the old lady told that actually the girl's father had contracted small pox and had died before he could fulfill the promise to visit the temple. Sugni's mother had also died earlier, leaving the two alone. She was looking for a match for her, she added. A little later we saw the trident with a red cloth on the temple and everyone started talking simultaneously.

We jumped off the boat and took a bath in the Ganges. My grandmother made puris and kheer, and after we had offered the bhog to the goddess along with flowers, a saree, and some money, she made me serve food to about twenty beggars sitting in a row. We walked around in the fair which was being held near the temple, and saw women lying prostrate, getting up, and again lying prostrate, proceeding to the temple. Some of them had come from as far as several tens of kilometers, travelling in this manner, over several days. There were a bunch of people with fearsome moustaches, carrying guns, complete with belts of bullets, who brought decorated plaques, covered with currency notes and sarees to the goddess. I looked at my grandmother and smiled, she smiled back to acknowledge that they were the famed dacoits of the area, come to pray. The fair was very crowded. I and my grandmother held on to each other but we lost Sugni and the old lady in the rush. We searched for them for a while, and returned to the ghat to take a boat back to the town.

It turned out to be the same boat by which we had gone. The boatmen told the story of my escape from the crocodile and the bravery of Sugni, to all the passengers. Where was she-I wondered, and tired, I fell asleep. My grandmother woke me when we reached the town. We got off the boat and came to the railway station to wait for the train.

It was almost midnight when the train came, as it was several hours late. It was then that I noticed two men with guns coming in with a girl, whose face was covered with her saree. They boarded a compartment and ordered everybody off. One of them hissed to the girl to keep her face covered and not to make any sound. Even before the train started, we could hear the screams of the girl tearing through the walls of the compartment and reaching us in the next compartment, which had become very crowded. No one took any notice. I looked at my grandmother and she just said, "Yes, she is Sugni".

When I grew restless, my grandmother told me the following; she had guessed it all along. The old lady was too soft spoken to be a farmer's wife, bringing up an orphaned girl. There were hardly any marks of hard work on her palms. She had perhaps "stolen" the girl when she was still very young, and had surely sold her to those men. Did my grandmother conjure this up to take my and also her mind off the incident or did the men with guns snatch Sugni from a poor, weak, old woman, come to fulfill her promise to the goddess of small pox? I do not know to this day. Only Mother Ganges and goddess Shitala know. However, I do remember that by the time my grandmother had finished, my wound had started throbbing and I had winced with pain.

Thirty years later, it is only a scar. Yet, there are nights when I am awakened by a scream and a fear that my right arm is missing.

11

Daughters

I first met Rahman during the heady days of 1972, when he came to Bombay as a member of a delegation from the newly born Bangla Desh. As other members of the delegation were quite elderly, we became good friends within days as I traveled with them around the city. I took them to art galleries, book shops, Elephanta Caves, and Kanheri Caves. We went around looking for a particular brand of hair oil-popular in Calcutta, stacks of colourful bindis, records of Rabindra Sangeet, Hindustani classical music, and Hindi film songs, silk sarees and khadi kurtas. We went around in search of authentic Benarasi paans after gorging on pani puris and sri khand. We parted with promises to keep in touch.

He kept his promise and in a few months I got an invitation to visit the University of Dhaka. The visit had to be postponed twice. It was finally abandoned, when in the middle of preparations for my visit, his country was once again plunged into chaos as the President of his country got killed. We, however, remained in touch through occasional letters.

And then we met in a city on the Adriatic coast in Italy. He was accompanied by his wife, who spoke some Urdu and who tried to teach me Bangla. Our friendship took off again, where we had left it earlier. We would walk together for hours along tree-lined avenues, admiring the statues and buildings, looking at expensive watches, jewellery, dresses and electronic equipments in the windows of the shops. And then we would sit in one of the numerous pizzerias for a dinner. The bindi and saree of his wife, her good looks, her dazzling smile and her pleasant personality made us quite popular and we were often joined by people on our table-enquiring about India and Bangla Desh and football, and suggesting that we visit Venice, Rome, and Florence before leaving Italy.

We celebrated Diwali together with some Pakistani and Indian students. I was greatly moved when two days later, on the Bhatra Dwitiya day his wife tied a rakhee on my hand. She had spent the previous evening making laddus and rosgollas. After a heavy meal we sat in his balcony, overlooking the Adriatic. We watched as little boats came to their moorings into the harbor, their sails fluttering, and the reflections of their lights dancing on the waves raised by the breeze. I casually told Rahman's wife that her name Kulsum reminded me of my cousin sister who was named Kusum.

Rahman struggled to control his emotions and Kulsum wept openly. I was completely confused. Were they unhappy that my affection for them was incomplete? Or they were unhappy that I needed the excuse of a name to tell that we were different? Was Kulsum thinking that my distant cousin was dearer to me than her, who sat in front of me, in flesh and blood, and who had struggled for a day to prepare a lavish meal, complete with sweets, in a foreign land?

The truth, told between sobs and long silences-broken by hoots of the distant boats, was far stranger. Kulsum's parents had lived near Central Calcutta and belonged to a reasonably well to do family of sweet-shop-owners. They owned a chain of sweet-shops, Ghosh Mosai located in almost all the areas of Calcutta. She was about six years old when a large group of people brandishing iron rods had attacked their shop during the Great Calcutta Killings. From a little opening in the window of her neighbours' house she had seen her parents and her brother being killed and then the shop being burnt.

Her neighbours, the Khans, left the city for Dhaka, before the teams seeking revenge arrived. They took her with them. They made some feeble attempt to locate her relatives in Calcutta and having failed, they brought up Kusum Ghosh, for that was her name, as Kulsum Khan. They had no children of their own and slowly Kulsum had filled that void, celebrating various festivals and fasting with them during Ramazans. She learnt to recite Koran well and grew up to be very popular among the relatives of her foster parents.

Still, there were occasions when she would have images of Durga Puja, Kali Puja, and Holi fleeting across her mind. The Khans did live in fear of her being exposed as a former Hindu during the independence movement for Bangla Desh, and only the thought of her being married into the influential family of Rahman had given them a measure of assurance.

I cursed myself for not being observant, as I recalled an incident which had taken place only a few days earlier. I and Kulsum were walking in a park, while Rahman had sauntered off to buy a packet of cigarettes. I had pointed to a basil plant and expressed a surprise that Vilayeti Tulasi was growing so abundantly there. She had stopped to cover her head with her saree and touched it with a reverence which has given strength to millions of Hindu women over centuries. Not knowing her back ground then, I had commented that only the conch shell and the lamp was missing!

Rahman joked that he had acquired a Hindu sala (brother-in-law). And this simple statement suddenly lifted the weight off our hearts and we laughed till Kulsum cried again, this time with joy.

I also did not know then that a little known Hindi film had earlier explored the mind of a Hindu girl Kusum, brought up as Kulsum! However when I saw it years later, I silently saluted the spirit of art which imitated life so closely.

Several years passed and I moved to Calcutta. Rahman came to Calcutta a few times and promised to bring Kulsum along next time, every time.

Our children had started going to school and my wife had taken up job at a neighbouring school for kids. Domestic help had become essential. Most of the time, the maids were refugees from Bangla Desh. The phenomenon was so common that we never even bothered about knowing their back-ground. However, coming from Bombay we were, almost always, pleasantly surprised by the very artistic names of the maids who came to work for us. Our curiousity stopped there. We were busy.

On one such morning I was shouting at our son for writing so badly that even he could not read it afterwards. Our new maid, Arpita, was mopping the floor. When I left the room, she talked to our son and requested him to try harder. With anger and ridicule in his voice he asked her, 'How?' Holding the the mop in one hand Arpita copied a sentence of English in his note book. He picked up the note book and came running to us. We saw, her exquisite hand writing, perfect, cursive, effortless, and elegant.

For the first time we paid attention to Arpita. Slim, tall, fair, polite in speech, gentle in manner, and neat-even in her poor clothes. She had recently come from Bangla Desh with her husband. She was educated upto class twelve and her husband was a graduate. Her beauty was her biggest enemy in the new version of Bangla Desh, where her family regularly received 'suggestions' to sell its land. The Bangla Desh for which her father had fought and given his life, was lost in the quagmire of rising fundamentalism and the debris of a mosque demolished on a cold day some-where in North India.

They had to flee leaving all behind. From a land-owning farmers, having several heads of cattle and ponds of fish they became domestic servants, in a foreign land. Her husband was working as a driver and she was our maid. She wept, talking about her house which was burnt, her mother-in-law who had stood between her and the marauding crowds, to give her and her husband time to escape, and about her parents, whose where-abouts she did not know. She was grateful for the few square feet of land where she was allowed to make her hut near a stinking canal, using pieces of card board and plastic sheets.

Around this time Rahman came to Calcutta. And Kulsum accompanied him. They stayed at a hotel and paid us a visit. Kulsum stood in front of the little corner in our house where my wife has put some pictures of gods and where she burns incense sticks every day. Kulsum gazed at those pictures, transfixed, saying nothing, touching nothing, as waves of pain and suffering lashed across her face.

She told us that she wanted to locate the house of her childhood. I went with Rahman and Kulsum to try to find the area where she thought that her parents had lived. Her foster parents, the Khans had died several years earlier and had never given her details of the locality from where they had gone. They were wise people, they knew that such memories are best left buried. Her own memory was very sketchy and yet full of details, which had lost their meaning in the intervening decades.

After driving around the lanes of Central Calcutta for several hours we gave up. At her request I took them to the Dakhineswar Temple where she she stood outside, on the steps leading to the Ganges and gazed silently into a past, which was lost forever to her and where she could not go. We just kept quiet.

We returned home and sat down for a cup of tea. Arpita was helping my wife in the kitchen. I switched on the television to listen to the news. There was a commentary about some political parties talking about the influx of refugees from Bangla Desh. I commented casually that it was really a pity that even after so many years people in the Indian sub-continent were fighting in the name of religion. His answer surprised me. He said, emphatically and quite clearly that all these people were coming to India for a better living and for making money and that there was no persecution of minorities in his country.

Suddenly we heard a heart-rending scream. Arpita came roaring to the drawing room, a kitchen knife in hand. She was shouting, crying, and screaming all in the same breath.

While I and my wife struggled to silence her, Kulsum got up, wrapped the pallu of her saree around her neck and knelt in front of Arpita to touch her feet. Between sobs, she told, “My dear sister, in the name of Ma Kali, forgive my husband. He is but a man and will never know the pain of a daughter separated from her mother.” And the commotion died slowly.

Rahman wanted to leave but sat down when Kulsum told that she had recognised her parents' house and the little temple where she had gone every evening with her mother. She had not stopped us when we had passed that area as she had realized that some memories are best left buried, exactly as her foster parents had desired.

12

Requital

Christmas cards from Mary always reach us by the twentieth of December, every year. This year is no exception. We are also very happy that she writes that she will spend three months in Calcutta next year, working with a charitable organization for which she had worked for two years, more than fifteen years ago.

I wonder, how we came so close. After all, I had spent only a very little time with her. Just a few hours in my office in Calcutta, a few meetings at our house, and a few days at Oxford, where she had acted as my guide.

I had gone to Oxford after living for several years in Germany. Oxford, and for that matter England, reminded me so much of India. Occasionally broken pavements, red double-decker buses-like the ones I had used in Bombay, crowded trains-where people sat on their luggage, Indian ticket checkers, Sikh bus drivers, red letter-boxes, people driving on the left, restaurant names like Bombay Palace, Annapurna and Taj Mahal, everything reminded me of

India. And yes, for the first time after leaving India I was following every little mischievous comment, every little twist of the language which created the humour-as only the English language permits, and every little teasing which went on everywhere, all the time. It reminded me of the humourous and satirical and almost lyrical commentaries one hears in the crowded buses of Calcutta. And I rejoiced in all the tongues of Asia and Africa, leaving their quaint marks on the language.

And then there was Mary. She was assigned by my host to take me around after my lectures. She had first taken me for a walk along the river flowing along the city. It was a bright and sunny day in summer. People lying all around, enjoying the sun shine. We settled on the grass, under a huge Oak tree and slowly the bright sun-shine, the light breeze, and the smell of roses surrounded us. We talked about our work and our families. Mary talked of her parents and her six sisters who lived in Ireland. She described the humour of her father by recalling that he used to say that 'Ireland is such an exciting place to live; you see-you go out for a walk and when you return you can't find your house!'

I showed her pictures of my wife and children and talked of our life in Calcutta. She told that she had made a pledge that when she completed her Ph. D. she would spend two years in Calcutta working for a charitable organization. I talked about my fancy notions that 'the state' was responsible for its citizens while she talked of her simple resolve to do her bit for the poor of Calcutta. Why Calcutta? Her grand-father had lived and taught in Calcutta. He had died young and lay buried there. I invited her to stay with us if she ever came to Calcutta. We talked of the general feeling among Indians that officers and men of Irish origin were more tolerant of the freedom fighters.

We went to several book shops, selling new and old

books from all over the world. Looking at a stack of old books, I chanced upon an a copy of "Gitanjali, Song Offerings", gifted by "J. to Dearest Elizabeth, with love, Calcutta, August 10, 1923". As I held it in my hands and turned its pages, I wondered about the journey of that book from Calcutta to England, perhaps by ship, perhaps after the independence and to the books shop, perhaps after the death of Elizabeth. Who was J? Who was Elizabeth? Where did they live in Calcutta? How strongly did they feel about Tagore? I could see that the book was well read and carried notes in an elegant hand-writing in pencil, on the margins. Were they sad when they had to leave Calcutta or they were happy to go back home? The book occupies a prominent place on our book-shelf and has always given me hours of bliss, every time I have picked it up and rejoiced in its sublime lyrics, often accentuated by the comments of "Elizabeth". But that is another story.

We walked from one college to the other, savouring the historical sights and walking through huge libraries. Mary took me to a play at an open air theater, after my last lecture. A day later, I had gone back to Germany.

After our return to Calcutta, I sent her a card at Oxford. It was returned by the secretary telling that Mary had completed her Ph. D. and left the university. She had not left any forwarding address. I wondered a bit about her and got busy with our life.

The month of June in Calcutta is never pleasant. It was very hot and very humid. The breeze stood still and there was no power. Our office, designed for air-conditioning, was simmering. The generator down-stairs produced a lot of noise and smoke and a small amount of electricity to run just one fan and one tube-light in the rooms where we sat. We were sweating profusely. It was impossible to work, it was even impossible to gossip. We were all very ill at ease and snapped at every-body and every-thing. It was then that I got a message from our security officer that a 'Sister' from one of the hospitals for children wanted to see me. I was amused and asked him to send her in.

A little later the peon arrived with the 'Sister'. I looked up to see a giggling Mary. She ran into my arms. I found that our eyes had become very wet, by the time we sat down. She was wearing a saree of rough home-spun cotton, a blouse of even rougher cotton, and worn rubber sandals. She carried a shoulder-bag full of papers. And her face was crimson red with sweat and heat. And yet she was smiling as if she were sitting under a oak tree at Oxford, on the banks of a gently flowing river, the sun shining mildly, the breeze playing with her hair, and roses in full bloom, all around the meadows.

She had arrived several months earlier, spent some time learning Bangla and Hindi and rudimentary nursing, and had been very busy. She had lost our home address but remembered the name of the institute. She had tried to call me several times but had not succeeded in reaching me. Ultimately she had decided to take the long and torturous bus journey, from the suburb in the far south of the city to reach me after changing buses thrice and traveling for three hours, when she had a day off.

We went to the cafeteria and took a thali. She used her fingers to eat the badly cooked rice-which was not even cleaned properly, with over-spiced vegetables and a watery dal, from a battered and dented steel plate, sipping water from an ill shaped steel glass.

I looked at her and remembered the sumptuous dinner, beginning with sherry and ending with cognac, at the high table of one of the colleges of Oxford, where my host was a don. Yes, the crockery was the finest bone-china and the cutlery solid-silver. The meal had included grilled salmon, roast suckling pig, and wild duck. The wine was a most satisfying red and the desert had just melted in our mouth infusing every one of our taste buds with pleasure. Yes I remember that evening. Mary had worn a dress of ethereal blue. The topaz necklace around her beautiful neck had accentuated her ocean-blue eyes. And her fingers had danced on the piano to relieve us of the misery of a pseudo-intellectual discussion about how ancient Romans shaved, as they had no safety razors! I remembered telling her that she had reminded me of a portrait of Jeanne Samary by Renoir.

Returning to the present, I apologized for the quality of the food. But she smiled and said that the food was actually far better than what she usually got. She was quite busy then with several children lined up for a medical check-up but promised to come to our house in a month's time when she was to have another day off. We tried to keep in touch by shouting across bad phone-lines and giving up when we could not scream any further.

A month later, she came to our house. Again, there was no power and she climbed to our seventh floor apartment in darkness. We opened the door to find a smiling Mary, a huge pot of rasgollas in her hands, sweating from head to toe. My wife gave her one of her sarees and she took a shower. We sat down for a meal, joking about having a candle-light dinner.

Our children were still very young and spoke just a few words of English. Soon they felt left out of our conversation, became quite noisy, giggling at their own little mischief and tried to draw our attention, by indulging in mock fights, and getting off the dining table and running around it. Suddenly Mary put her knife and fork aside and reached out for her handkerchief.

'Is the food very hot?' my wife asked. 'No, no, no' she replied between sobs. And then she added, 'Working with spastic and retarded children for the last eighteen months, I had forgotten that the laughter of normal children can give us so much joy and that they can be so lively.'

We finished the meal in silence. The children went to bed and we shifted to the balcony where a whisper of a breeze was reaching. Mosquito repellent coils were quite useless against them and they feasted upon us and yet Mary did not complain. We sat and talked late into the night. She talked of her work with the children and of her boy-friend who had moved to Michigan and perhaps away from her. She talked of the offer she had from New Zealand to teach at a college. And she talked of the frustration that her father could never reach her by phone. 'The first thing I will do when I get back home', she said, 'is to call friends, just to hear their voices-clearly over the phone!'

I asked her if she had found the grave of her grand-father and she told that she had met the current priest of the church which he had frequented and found the record of his burial at one of the cemeteries. She was planning to go there, the next day. We purchased flowers and accompanied her.

With the help of a very old photograph and the priest, we located the badly damaged grave. We could see that the marble lining, the angels, and the larger pieces of stone seen in the photograph were gone. The bricks were falling from the sides. Looking around we found a piece of marble. We could read 'aul Bryan' on it. Patrick Paul Bryant was her grand-father and we realized that the stone could have come from his grave. While I and my wife were fuming with rage at the desecration, Mary expressed a great delight and excitement at the discovery and joked about the 'luck of the Irish!' We left the flowers at the grave and returned home.

She visited us a few times again to play with our

children and to 'recharge her batteries', in her own words.

A few months later her assignment was over. She decided to visit her family for Christmas, before taking up the job in New Zealand. We did not hear for a long from her.

And then during Christmas we received a card from her from Auckland. It contained a small note on a separate sheet of paper. Her father had proved prophetic. It was the New Year's Eve. They were waiting for dinner to be served when he had noticed that he had run out of cigars. Mary had offered to go and buy them from a shop in the neighborhood. She had returned to find a crater where her house had stood just ten minutes earlier. Her entire family was blown to pieces, almost like the grave of her grand-father-she had added almost as an after-thought.

She further wrote that her 'Irish luck' still held as she had left a photograph of her family with us, which was the only one surviving now. She had asked us to send it to her along with a piece of stone from her grand-father's grave.

We went to the cemetery, but could not find any trace of the damaged grave. Even the bricks were gone and just a shallow pit marked the approximate location of the grave. I looked at my wife, thought for a second, and picked a small piece of stone from a grave near-by, which was falling to pieces. We sent that with the photograph with a hope that Mary would not know the difference and that gods will forgive us for this deception.

And now we have a worry. Will Mary see through the deception we created for her, when she comes to Calcutta-the deception that we offered her in return for the service to the people of our city? In fact, we realize that we had never visited her at the hospital at which she had worked.

13

The Yellow Villa

Most of the cultivated land in our village belongs to the Thakur of the Peeli Kothi or 'The Yellow Villa'. Madhav, the famous folk singer of the village had composed a melodious song about the beauties of the Peeli Kothi and the generosity of the Thakur. He was given a turban and fifty rupees in the good old days of fifties, when he sang the song in the presence of the Thakur during one of the gatherings to celebrate the festival of Holi. And this song was used by the boys of our village when they wanted to tease kids from other villages. Yes, that song had the aura of our 'village anthem'.

It was the only house in the village which was made of bricks. All other houses had mud walls with thatched or tiled roofs. There were whispers that even if others could afford it, they would not build a house of bricks, for the fear of the Thakur.

It was a huge house, rising to three storeys, with a

vast terrace on the roof where the Thakur and his family slept during summer and from where one could see the entire village. There was a huge mango orchard around the Villa and a large garden in front, with beds of roses, jasmine, and mogra flowers, and a long row of palms leading to the court-yard. The pathways in the lawn were paved with concrete and washed with care. You could walk for hours there and not dirty your feet. The manicured lawn had several wrought iron structures covered with ivy and flowering creepers and which looked like exotic animals. The lawn alone had an area which was several times the land holdings of most of the villagers, who were essentially labourers in the fields of the rich farmers. Our village also supplied work-force to the cities as far away as Calcutta and Bombay. If you have an avid ear, you can hear the nuances of the dialects of our village in the speech of the cart-pullers and unskilled labourers of these cities.

Yes, the richness of the Thakur was visible everywhere. The terrace was full of plants in huge flower pots, which were in turn kept in still more huge brass vessels having floral designs. There were only a few houses in the village which had brass cooking vessels. The cooking vessels in most of the households consisted of an iron plate, tawa, to make chapatis and an aluminum vessel to cook the occasional dal.

It was said that if the Thakur sold the brass pots on his terrace, he could feed the entire village for several days! If you could climb to the topmost branch of the old mangoe tree behind the villa, you could see the brass pots beautifully polished and shining like gold.

A large body of men and women worked in the house-hold, cleaning the rooms, the furniture, and the vast grounds. They polished the brass and took care of the farm animals, milked the cows, churned the curd to make ghee, and carried out millions of domestic chores. The Thakur, sat in the court yard pulling at his hukka-the hubble-bubble. A servant kept watch on the fire and the scented tobacco. If the Thakur decided to have a walk, the servant followed him, a few feet behind, the hukka in hand, proffering it to him when ever he desired it. On such occasions, the Thakur just extended his hand and the servant ran to put the pipe in his hands.

The Thakur had two grades of servants, ones who worked in the fields, and the others who worked in his house-hold. The workers in the field could go up to the cattle-shed to feed the oxen and to fetch them for ploughing, or grazing, or other farm works. The other and socially higher grade of servants worked in the house-hold. They told several stories about the wealth in the villa. One of the stories was that during the Great Mutiny, Nana Shaheb Peshwa had stayed incognito in a house belonging to the ancestors of the Thakur and his followers had paid them handsomely to stop them from handing him over to the British. Another story hinted that the ancestor was a lover of one of the Begums of Lucknow and he got valuable gifts from her including the money to buy the village.

We could go up to the court-yard during the Holi, when the entire village went to pay respects to the Thakur. They were served marijuana, bhang, sweets on solid silver plates, 'sherbet' in solid silver glasses, and paan. They sang bawdy songs, playing drums and cymbals, while the servants of the Thakur sprayed them with coloured and perfumed water from a sprinkler of solid silver.

In fact I always associated the Yellow Villa with scents, so pleasing and so different from the smell of cow-dung, rotting vegetation, and dirty ponds, which pervaded the rest of the village. I also admired the sprinkler, its silver shining with only a hint of coloured water on the handle. It had a beautiful engraving of a powerful lion attacking a large elephant. During these festivities, the people would go one by one to the Thakur, applying a little bit of abeer on his fore-head or to his feet. Every year the village grocery shop sold abeer of one colour to the rest of the villagers and of a different colour to the Thakur, which was sold only to him and to no one else.

I remember standing there and wondering at all the wealth in the middle of the surrounding squalor and poverty and deprivation. Yes, this sure must have been the result of the wonderful deeds of the Thakur in his previous birth, I had concluded.

During the rains, the Thakur organized recitations from the Bhagavat and we went there to listen to the stories from the life of Lord Krishna. He also organised the Ram Leela during Dussehra and a dangal (wrestling match) during the Nag Panchami. There were people who remembered receiving upto one hundred rupees as a prize from the Thakur on such occasions.

Yes, he was a generous man. He rode a huge black horse, its coat glistening with sweat when he rode it. The older boys told us that his horse ran faster than the Punjab Mail, the train which passed our village every day, around noon. A number of servants were constantly taking care of the horse, cleaning chick-pea to feed it, scrubbing it, and giving it a thumping massage. They were to run leaving all work at hand to remove the droppings the moment the horse produced it. There was also a custom in our village that the marriage parties coming to the houses of rich farmers would bring some elephants and horses with them. This used to excite us considerably as it was sure to result in a horse race, which the visitors invariably lost. I remember one occasion when a mare accompanying a marriage party had defeated the black horse. It was seen limping, the next day.

The Thakur also owned several guns which were regularly oiled, fired, and kept in a fine condition. There were always some young men, well built, exercising in a shed in the villa, practising stick-fights, and occasionally shooting. As children we would some-times go to watch them, exercising, their well-built bodies glistening with sweat. They were guards of Yellow Villa. One often heard stories of robberies in neighbouring villages, none ever took place in our village. Well, almost none till the great robbery at the house of Gangu Teli, the oil-seed-crusher of the village.

The family of Gangu was rumoured to be very rich. He bought grain during the harvest and took it to the mandis, or stored it and sold later. He would buy mustard and other oil yielding seeds and crush them to get oil. He would buy hemp and get people to make ropes and strings to be sold. And he sold grocery to the village. Yet he always lived frugally, dressed poorly, and talked most politely. Gangu had only one son who was of marriageable age and in due course of time he was married.

When the dowry arrived we assembled to have a look. There were silver plates and glasses, gold ornaments, expensive sarees, and dry fruits. We could only make a guess about the cash amount he had received as a part of the dowry. The estimates varied from five to ten hundred thousand rupees. The reason was also not hard to find. The bride limped as she walked and had a face covered with pock-marks. She was not particularly attractive in spite of her youth. She was good natured though, and she sat in the grocery shop giggling at us from behind her veil when we asked for some groceries.

Villagers do not have much use of beauty, a good

hard working and sincere person is far more valued. She soon became popular and her mother-in-law started telling around that the young girl was very lucky for them. Was is to silence the critics who whispered that her husband had yielded to wealth?

Let me return to the story of the Thakur. He had started taking a special interest in my studies after I stood first in the district in the final examination of class five. He gave a personal scholarship of five rupees a month to me. The scholarship was a great help to me as I could pay my fees and buy books. This stopped my father from badgering me to leave school to help him in the fields. I had to go to Yellow Villa every month to collect the scholarship. I would wish him respectfully from a distance and he would ask me about the progress of my studies and remind me that I had to stand first again in the district in the examinations for the Junior High School. I was to protect the ijjat (honour) of the village, which was also his ijjat.

It is very difficult for me to explain to you, but his house was the only place where there were a few books and where a weekly newspaper arrived by mail. The paper always arrived on Saturdays and I went to his house on Sunday morning to read it to him and to some people who gathered in his court-yard to hear the news. Often, I was stopped in mid-sentence so that they could discuss or comment on the news. And this was the only time when I got to read anything other than my books.

Slowly the Thakur house-hold developed some fondness for me and some-times I was called into the zenana (the inside of the house, where the women lived). Ranijee, as the wife of the Thakur was called, was a pretty lady. She sat on a couch, smelling of perfumes, slowly chewing a paan, a maid servant in attendance, either fanning her or just waiting upon her. She had a book called Prem Sagar about the life of Lord Krishna. She would ask me to read it to her and would reward me with milk or sweets. My own mother had died when I was very young and my Grandmother had brought me up. I had never known the affection of a mother before; only an indulgence of a Grandmother. Yes, I remember those days. The book was written in the dialect of Braj Bhasha spoken around Vrindavan and Mathura and had a sweetness of its own. This coupled with the sweetness of the naughty mischief of Krishna as a child and then as a lover of gopis made a very powerful narrative. The story was really very well told and discussed at length the sadness of the Yamuna River, the sadness of trees, the sadness of cows who would not graze, the grieving of the villagers of Gokul, and the grief of Nature after Krishna left Vrindavan. The Ranijee would sob openly when I read that and ask me to read it again.

It was around this time that we heard that all was not well in the Thakur house-hold. As I was a regular visitor there, people often asked me in whispers if I had seen or heard of some argument. I only knew that the son of the Thakur lived in the city of Allahabad and was rumoured to live in a big house full of servants. It was also rumoured that he engaged in gambling and often lost heavily. Then he would come to the village and cajole his mother and argue with his father for more money. He talked of setting up of large factories and business houses, away from the mud and mosquitoes of the village, but he had neither the stamina nor the drive to carry out any of the plans. He was a handsome young men somewhat wasted due to the excessive indulgence in alcohol and women of ill-repute. He was perhaps not much more than twenty five but looked much older.

He had come home for a visit, and asked his father for a large sum of money, which he had refused. There was some shouting and then he had left in a huff.

Yes, I remember that night. It was a moon-less night and quite cold. My father and Grandmother had gone to Allahabad for a dip at the confluence of the Ganges and the Yamuna rivers. It was late in the night and I was studying in my room, which was the outermost in our house. I heard a few shots and shouting. It was not difficult for me to guess that the noise came from the direction of Gangu Teli's house. I heard him shouting for help, I heard his wife screaming for help, I heard his son and daughter-in-law screaming for help. But no one came forward. A robbery was in progress. Later we heard that the robbers, their faces covered with cloth had beat Gangu up, had beat his son up and had proceeded to strip his wife and daughter-in-law. And then he had given them the keys of his chests and the store room.

I dimmed the wick of the lantern, almost cutting off the light completely and came out of my room which had no windows. I looked in the direction of Gangu's house. I could hear the muffled shouts of the robbers giving directions to each other. And then I saw the outline of a man on a horse some distance away. And I saw the men running away towards the river bed. I watched the man on the horse turn, and proceed towards our house. I got scared. I ran inside my room and extinguished the lantern. I heard the sound of a horse running past and then a big thud followed by a painful neighing of the horse and cursing by the rider. There was no mistake. In a few minutes the son of the Thakur was in my room. I got up and lighted the lantern again. He was in pain and had broken his arm. I dimmed the light, and he lay in my bed. People were not yet coming out of their houses. I ran to the Yellow Villa. The gate was open and though very late, the Thakur was up, reading some-thing. Even though the servant who looked after his hukka tried to stop me, I pushed him quietly aside and walked up to him, closing the door behind me. He looked up. And understood. 'Has any one else seen him going to your house', he asked. I shook my head. He asked me to stay in his house till my father returned.

Some men appeared. And they were dusty and sweating, even though it was cold. They went to our house and brought the young Thakur on a cot. The elder Thakur looked at one of the men and said, 'Chote (young) Thankur had an argument with me and took the horse to work off his anger. He got injured.' That is what we heard the next day-the day when people talked of the fight between the Thakur and his son and about the robbery at Gangu Teli's house. Later in the day I was taken to see the horse, which had started limping, shot.

Next day my father returned and came to meet the Thakur. He told my father that the atmosphere of the village was no longer good and that my Grandmother was getting very old and was often sick. He had decided to send me to a boarding school in Shimla. He asked me to go in and take leave from Ranijee. I went in. Ranijee called me to her room and closed the door. She told me that she had begged Thakur Saheb to spare my life and that she was asking me to save the honour of the Yellow Villa. And then she wiped the tears welling up in her eyes. That was the last I saw them.

Next day, one of the servants of Thakur took me to Shimla with a letter from him. I joined the boarding school. Every month a money order arrived which covered my fees and living expenses till I completed my college education and joined the Indian Police Service. I could never return even during vacations. My father came to meet me there. One day he brought the news of my Grandmother's death. He quietly added that the Thakur had forbidden him to call me.

My father sold his little land holding and came to live with me. Once in a while I would get some news of the village.

One day I was sent to Allahabad. I was sitting with the In-charge of a Police Station and taking a stock of the law and order of the area as the festivals of Holi and Muharram were falling in the same week, that year. Our discussion was disturbed by the shouting of constables who brought in a man, who was cursing them in English. They said they had caught him selling stolen silver vessels.

I looked at the vessels. Even though, no longer shining, I recognized the silver sprinkler used so often in the Yellow Villa to spray scented and coloured water on the guests. I had never forgotten the intricate and elegant design of a powerful lion attacking a large elephant on that sprinkler. And I looked at the remaining vessels. Among them was a set of seven glasses of solid silver. A fine engraving in elegant and flowing Dev Nagri on each of them read -'On the occasion of the auspicious wedding of Rama Chadra Teli, son of Ganga Prasad Teli'.

I looked up from my desk and saw the Chote Thakur; dirty, scared, and broken. I do not know if he recognized me in his drunken state. However I do remember that I felt a gentle breeze rise in the room. It reminded me of the perfumed sarees of Ranijee and of the scented tobacco which Thakur used to smoke; both of whom had died some years earlier.

I told the constables to ask him to leave with his bag of silver vessels.

14

The New Silk Route

When I was young, I always asked for a window-seat during flights. I would sit for hours watching the clouds, as the plane passed below them, through them and above them. The ground seen from above was always a lot more beautiful, the fields always looked green, the deserts never looked forbidding, and the snow on the mountains always symbolized purity. The distances hid the poverty, the ugly scars, the fights, and the sufferings. I always liked my flights to Europe, which some-times followed the silk-route. I would travel hundreds of miles in an hour at a height of several thousand feet, covering the distances which the ancient caravans took months to cover. And I would wonder about those brave men who went from one end of the earth to the other end, in search of adventure and trade and to spread the words of messiahs. And I would wonder about the goods they carried. And I would wonder about the armies of Huns and Greeks and Mongols and Turks and Arabs racing along, conquering, capturing, destroying, and building.

And I would wonder about the large number of slaves these wars always produced who would be uprooted from their native soil and taken to a foreign land, only to perish with-out leaving a trace. And I would wonder, if some of them were cousins of my ancestors. I suppose, I wanted to feel pain and yet feel lucky that my own ancestors escaped their fate, or else I would have been borne-if at all in some other land. I say 'if at all', because not infrequently these souls were sold after being neutered. How did they manage in a land with different gods, different customs, and a different language? Did they retain the memories of their land, say in some songs. How quickly were they integrated and lost in the new world? And the women? What happened to them? Did any of the women taken by Mahmud of Gajani or Taimur leave any record or a tale any-where? Did the slaves taken by the Mongols from one end of the earth to the other end ever retain their memory? Can I find any trace of their existence in those foreign lands, if I visit there?

With passage of time, I have come out of this self-inflicted regimen of self-pity and unhappiness. Now I prefer an aisle seat, so that I can move about easily. I just sit, close my eyes and listen, or just observe.

The flight to London had started in Dhaka and when I boarded it in Kolkata I found my seat occupied. I looked at the occupant. He wore an ill-fitting and crumpled suit. He had half-tucked a large jute bag some-how below the seat in front of him and he sat with a great difficulty, squeezing his legs between his seat and the bag. And he looked scared. I found an empty seat and sat down and closed my eyes to savour the dialects of Bangla which I hear, but only rarely now, in the houses of my friends whose parents came from East Bengal or from our maid who recently came from Bangla Desh.

They talked longingly of fish, and mangoes, and ripe

jack-fruit, and leechees, and relatives, and river boats, and songs which they were leaving behind to live in England, working as cooks and helpers and cleaners and shop attendants. The better dressed ones were perhaps white-collar workers as they maintained a look of bored indifference to all these talks and tried their best to look as if they did not belong to this motley crowd.

The flight was rather odd as they served break-fast and nothing else till we reached London, when they served lunch. The seasoned travelers walked to the back and collected some sand-witches. But most of the people just sat quietly and endured the hunger.

The composition of the crowd changed completely after London. The air-hostesses kept moving about with baskets of sand-witches and trays of drinks continuously. The lady sitting next to me was returning from Poland, after a successful drive to recruit young Polish students to work in her holiday-resort in Alabama where rich American parents sent their children to hunt and to trek. Her Polish 'brigade' was to keep the rooms clean. She had discovered over years that even after she paid for their travel from Poland to USA and back and paid for their food, lodgings, and some pocket money, it was cheaper for her to hire them than to hire American boys and girls, even at the minimum wages. And of-course these Polish boys were so hard working and grateful to her; they loved her dearly and came back year after year, introducing their younger siblings and friends to her when they took full-time jobs.

I reached North Carolina. A lot of construction was going on in the University. I am an early riser and yet while I walked to the University, I would meet the stocky and short Mexican men who had already put in an hour or more of work, who would smile, and continue with their hard labour of shifting materials and construction. At the sites which were isolated they would even sing while working. Every day on the television, I would listen to discussions about illegal immigrants, sustaining the economies of the Southern States by their hard work under difficult working conditions. I would hear stories of their willingness to accept salaries which were much less than the minimum wages, and to work without any insurance. These illegal workers got paid in cash and kept their savings with them, which made them an easy target for muggings and murders. They paid handsome amounts to 'coyotes'-the agents who transported them to USA hidden in trucks, under cover of darkness, chased, sometimes, by ferocious guard dogs and armed border police. And I listened to the complaints that English may be replaced by Spanish in these states, as the 'browning' of the USA continued.

My stay at the University came to an end, and it was time for me to return. The route included San Francisco airport, where I met a large number of Sikhs, on their way to India. Loaded with heavy luggage, they reminded me of the people going from Dhaka to London. As they spoke little English, I offered to help them and they attached themselves to me. I found that they were working in farms and factories owned by Sikhs in USA and Canada. Some of them were employed by the owners of restaurants and petrol stations. I learnt that the pay for working with hazardous substances was higher in USA. When we reached Tokyo, we were joined by a large number of Thai workers, returning to Bangkok. I looked at them and tried to discern the difference between them and the people from Dhaka, and Poland, and Mexico, and Punjab. I failed to find any.

Back to Kolkata on my drive back to Salt Lake, I

passed by Ultadanga. It was quite early in the morning. I saw a large number of labourers standing there waiting to be hired as daily workers. The labour contractors were selecting the stronger ones, leaving out the rest. They looked blankly at some far off point, not even murmuring that they might go hungry, if they did not get a job.

Suddenly I heard a heart-rending scream. It was coming from my bag. I unzipped it and discovered that the silk saree I had bought in Thailand was dripping with blood. I hastily threw it into a garbage dump. Somehow it became unfurled and I had a very clear vision; as clear as this paper you're reading. I saw slaves toiling in the ancient silk and carpet factories of Thailand, China, and Persia to keep the traffic on the silk-route flowing.

15

In Search of a Poem

There was a time when I wrote poems, lots of them. Perhaps I was more sensitive then, or perhaps I was not yet cynical. I still scribble a few lines occasionally and then I tear-up the sheets of paper. When I told this to my friends, one of them suggested that it might help if I relived the situations when I wrote poems.

I looked at the collection of my poems. I read them one by one and recalled the circumstances when I had written them, indulging shamelessly in the pleasures of nostalgia. And then it slipped out from the bunch of loose clippings; my first poem. I looked at the date. It was published almost twenty-five years ago.

And I recalled. I lived in Bombay then, in the suburbs near Ghatkopar East. The area was under development and the low-lying land was being slowly filled up. During high tides, sea-water from the back-bay along the Ghatkopar-Thane highway, beyond which the New Bombay was being developed, came to the boundary wall of our housing complex. When the moon was up, we sat in the balcony looking at the vast stretch of water, glistening like molten silver. When the water receded, equally vast stretches of small bushes would surface where birds looked for crabs and dead fish during the day, and where they nested near occasional boulders.

There was a little culvert on the road connecting our complex to the main road. This marshy land stretched as far as the eyes could see on the left. There was a mini-lagoon surrounded on the three sides by houses on the right. The culvert brought the seawater to the lagoon during high tide and drained it when the tide was low, leaving a small pool. I used to work till late in the library and while returning I used to get off the bus to walk the last kilometre along the marsh. This always had a very calming effect on me, as I went over the happenings during the day.

Then one evening I saw the family. Father, mother, and three young boys; the eldest with a large cut mark on his forehead. They had cleared an area of about six feet by six feet on the edge of the road on the mini-lagoon. They had spread a worn mat, on which the children sat with their father. The mother had put a few stones together and started a fire. I could see some rice being cooked. The rest of their belongings were kept in a metallic box with peeling paint. It was not hard for me to see that the family had seen better days, but a severe famine was razing across Maharashtra and every day it pushed a horde of landless labourers to the city.

I started seeing this family every day. The children went around with gunny-bags, picking up paper, pieces of metal, plastic bags. It was then that I started writing the poem. "Have you ever looked for a scrap of paper, a piece of junk, in garbage dumps? How would you ever understand the meaning of eureka?"

The mother started working as a maid in one of the many apartments in the neighbourhood. The father, after some misadventures started a small, very small teashop where the construction workers came to take tea. They sat on the roadside on small boulders of stone or on their haunches, sipped tea, stretched their limbs and left to work again. Slowly a small hut was built. Lest you have any romantic notions-this hut was a simple affair, made of sheets of plastics, beaten tin cans and scraps of wood. And I continued with the poem. "Have you ever constructed a hut-using plastic bags, tin cans and pieces of discarded plywood? How can you ever gauge the magnificence of the Taj Mahal?"

You know the rains of Bombay-relentless and heavy, without break for days. The family would just sit there, the roof leaking from every corner, the roadside flooding and water-stinking, dirty and laden with the garbage of the city entering the hut, the tea-shop closed as there would be no construction. And I wrote, "Have you ever heard the rumble of hungry intestines? How do you think, you can ever know the divinity of Raga Jaijaivanti?"

Then one night, returning very late, I heard muffled sounds of lovemaking coming from the hut, as I walked past. I felt as if I was violating their privacy, and yet I wrote, "Have you ever made love to a woman-always coughing, always sick, always tired, always scratching her unwashed hair, matted and full of lice? How would you know the charm of the heroines of Kalidasa?"

I added some homilies about inequalities and frustrations and the poem was complete. To my surprise, it was accepted by the very first magazine, to which I submitted it. I felt a kind of gratitude to the family for having been the source of inspiration. So I would smile at the children when I met them on the road, or occasionally acknowledge the man running the teashop. The construction work started again and the business at the teashop picked up. They bought a broken table and started supplying, first cheap biscuits, then bread, and then omelets with the tea. There was a boom in the construction business in the area and the shop just expanded. The children stopped picking rags and started helping the father and then the mother also started helping him, leaving her job as a maid. The hut started looking sturdier.

And then one day I noticed an idol of Ganesha in a corner of the shop. It was a most unusual idol, of polished marble, about a foot in size. A baby Ganesha was crawling towards a plate full of "laddoos" and had a "laddoo" in one of his hands, about to eat it. The expressions were very clear and the whole depiction had a very pleasing effect on me. By then I had developed a nodding acquaintance with the family. I stopped and inquired about the idol. I told them that I had seen such paintings involving baby Krishna but never Ganesha.

The father told that the idol was with the family for several generations, and one of his ancestors who used to be in the Maratha Army had got it specially made in Mathura, having seen a similar idol of Lord Krishna. I must confess that I felt a pride about my discerning eyes.

By now the teashop had picked considerably and the family had started keeping some provisions. Some more huts came up alongside and soon the area around the lagoon was converted into a small colony of huts, converting it to what the people in Bombay call a "Jhopad Patti". The people slowly reclaimed the lagoon and then it was gone. And it was time for me to move to Calcutta.

I decided to visit the area during my next visit to Bombay. In fact I realized that I had never been there after leaving Bombay some twenty years ago. I got down at the bus stop where I used to, but could not recognize the rest of the place. The whole area was teeming with people and vehicles. Several high-rise buildings had come up, and there was no sign of the marsh. After some effort I found the old road, which was much widened now. A large multi-storied shopping complex occupied the space where the colony of the huts used to be. I felt confused at the loss of a part of my past. Yet, I wanted to linger there for a few more minutes. I decided to have a cup of coffee at a cafe in the complex.

As I sat down and looked up I saw the idol of Ganesha, neatly decorated, in a marble-lined alcove, with flowers and incense sticks. And I saw a framed-photograph of the father with a garland of "mogra" flowers and a "tilak" of fresh sandalwood paste on the forehead. I sat there, sipping the coffee and looked at the young-man at the counter, a large cut-mark on his forehead, busily counting money and ordering a number of waiters around.

I looked at the idol of Ganesha again. And I can bet that He winked at me. And then He smiled. It was a smile as poetic as a high tide in the Arabian Sea on a full moon. It was also a song in praise of the city of Bombay and a quiet determination of an unknown family, with a sense of pride. A family which, I recalled, had never complained: not when they slept in the open-by the side of road, not when the stinking waters of Bombay roads entered their makeshift hut, not when they sat without food and the rains poured over their heads. I also recalled that they had never asked anyone for any help. And I realized that the prose of a quiet determination is far more lyrical than the poetry of pity -which I had always penned.